CAT IN THE CA

Perplexed, Mandy looked around. The strange noise was coming from somewhere to her right. She lifted the lantern higher, trying to see what was there.

And then, in the soft glow given off by the candle, she noticed a rounded object bumping against the cottage wall. Intrigued, she leaned out over the edge of the porch to get a closer look.

'Oh! It's only an old barrel,' she said to herself, recognising the shape. She reached out to push the barrel away from the house but, as her hand caught hold of it, she saw a small movement inside.

And then she heard a faint sound.

'There's something in there!' Mandy exclaimed.

Quickly she pulled the barrel towards her. As it came into the candlelight she saw a pair of bright eyes staring up at her.

'It's a cat!' Mandy cried.

Animal Ark series

Holiday Specials

Plus

LUCY DANIELS

Cat
— in the —
Candlelight

Illustrations by Ann Baum

**Hodder
Children's
Books**

a division of Hodder Headline Limited

Special thanks to Andrea Abbott

Thanks also to C. J. Hall, B.Vet.Med., M.R.C.V.S., for reviewing the veterinary information contained in this book.

Animal Ark is a trademark of Working Partners Limited
Text copyright © 2002 Working Partners Limited
Created by Working Partners Limited, London W6 0QT
Original series created by Ben M. Baglio
Illustrations copyright © 2002 Ann Baum

First published in Great Britain in 2002
by Hodder Children's Books

For more information about Animal Ark,
please contact www.animalark.co.uk

10 9 8 7 6 5 4 3 2 1

A Catalogue record for this book is available from
the British Library

ISBN 0 340 85115 5

Typeset by Avon Dataset Ltd, Bidford-on-Avon, Warks

Printed and bound in Great Britain by
Clays Ltd, St Ives plc

Hodder Children's Books
a division of Hodder Headline Limited
338 Euston Road
London NW1 3BH

ANIMAL
ARK
VETERINARY
SURGERY

One

A sudden strong gust of wind almost knocked Mandy Hope off her bicycle. 'Yikes!' she exclaimed, feeling the bike wobble beneath her. She steadied herself and carried on down the lane.

The wind blew an icy sheet of rain into her face. For a moment Mandy was blinded. She blinked, then wiped her eyes with her arm. 'I'll be soaked by the time I get home,' she muttered to herself. 'Trust it to start raining like this just in time for the Christmas holidays!'

She swerved to avoid a big puddle, then

pedalled on as fast as she could. Before long, she could see the Animal Ark sign at the end of the lane. It stood out against the grey cloudy sky and swayed back and forth in the wind, its hinges creaking loudly. Relieved, Mandy whizzed beneath it and sped up the driveway to the old stone cottage where she lived.

Her father was standing in the doorway of the modern veterinary surgery that was attached to the back of the cottage. Mandy's parents were vets and they ran Animal Ark, in the Yorkshire village of Welford.

'Is that a drowned rat coming to be revived?' Adam Hope's cheerful voice called out, as Mandy jumped off her bike outside the shed in the back garden.

'Almost drowned, Dad,' Mandy called back. She wheeled her bike into the shed, shut the door, then ran across the soggy lawn towards the surgery. 'And the only thing that can revive me is a big mug of hot chocolate!'

'You're in luck there – your mum's just made some,' smiled Adam Hope as they went inside. 'Sorry you had to battle the elements to get home, love,' he continued, closing the door behind them.

'I'd have picked you up from school if we hadn't been so busy all morning.'

'That's OK, Dad,' Mandy said. She dumped her bag on the floor then took off her dripping raincoat and hung it on the coat-stand next to the door. 'And anyway, it only started raining when I was about halfway home.' Mandy's school was in the town of Walton, about two miles away.

Animal Ark's receptionist, Jean Knox, looked up from her computer. 'Let's hope it stops raining as quickly as it started,' she said. 'My grandchildren are coming to stay tomorrow. They'll be here until after Christmas, and the last thing I need is for them to be cooped up indoors.'

Adam Hope nodded and grinned sympathetically.

'Still, with any luck, all this wind will blow the rain away,' Jean went on, trying to sound positive.

'No chance of that, I'm afraid,' said Emily Hope, coming into the reception. She went over to Mandy and hugged her. 'Lucky it was the last day of term and you came out early, love. There's just been a warning on the radio about strong gales later on. And the weatherman said we're in for really severe conditions for at least the next few days.'

'Oh, no!' Mandy exclaimed, her voice filled with frustration. 'James and I were going to do some cross-country cycling in the woods this week.'

James Hunter was Mandy's best friend. He lived on the other side of Welford village.

'But I guess we can always wait until after Christmas,' Mandy continued. 'And in the meantime, I'll have loads of time to help out around here.'

Mandy had her regular duties at Animal Ark, like feeding sick and recovering animals in the residential unit and cleaning out their cages. But she was always ready to help out in other ways during her spare time.

'Well, if today's anything to go by, you'll be rushed off your feet,' said Adam Hope, checking the big blue appointment book on the desk.

'That's fine by me,' Mandy smiled.

'It's lucky for us that you're going to be around,' said Emily Hope. 'We've already admitted three animals to the residential unit today and they'll need plenty of attention.'

'I'll go and see to them as soon as I've changed out of these wet clothes,' Mandy said, looking down at her navy blue school trousers which clung to her legs. She turned to go into the cottage.

'Don't forget your hot chocolate,' Mr Hope called out after her. 'It's on the counter.'

'And there's a slice of pizza in the oven for your lunch,' added Emily Hope.

Mandy went into the kitchen, gulped down her hot chocolate, then, taking the pizza with her, ran upstairs to change.

Five minutes later, she returned to the reception room where a woman and her young daughter were waiting. On the bench between them was a travelling basket. Mandy remembered them from a previous visit when they'd brought in a cat. 'Hello, Mrs Wilson,' she said to the woman. Then, peering into the basket she asked the girl, 'Who have you got in here today, Beth?'

'Stardust,' said the child. 'She's not very well.'

Inside the basket was a silver-grey chinchilla. The little animal sneezed once then stared out at Mandy.

'Hello, pretty one,' Mandy said. Despite the warmth in the room, Stardust was shivering. 'You don't look very happy,' Mandy added.

'She hasn't eaten all day,' said Beth in a serious voice. 'And she sneezes like that a lot.' She pushed her fingers through the cage and stroked the

chinchilla's soft fur. 'But don't worry, Stardust, the vets will make you better.' She looked up anxiously at Mandy. 'They will, won't they?'

Mandy smiled at her. 'Of course,' she said, straightening up as her mum came out of the treatment room.

'You can bring Stardust in now,' said Emily Hope to Mrs Wilson. 'Oh, and Mandy, will you give me a hand please? Simon's helping Dad with an injured puppy.'

Simon was the practice nurse. He had been at

Animal Ark for about three years.

'What happened to the puppy?' asked Mandy, following her mum into the treatment room.

'He managed to get his head stuck in a gate,' Mrs Hope told her. 'It's taken his owners almost an hour to get him out so he's pretty bruised and upset.'

Mandy winced, thinking how the puppy must have struggled to free himself.

In the treatment room, Mandy took Stardust out of her basket and put her on the table so that Mrs Hope could examine her. The chinchilla sneezed again several times, then lay so listlessly that Mandy didn't even need to hold her still.

'She's completely exhausted,' said Mrs Hope. She listened to Stardust's chest through her stethoscope. 'She's battling to breathe,' she remarked. 'And this nasal discharge isn't a good sign.' She listened a little longer, then removed the stethoscope and said to Mrs Wilson, 'Stardust's got a respiratory disease. I'll give her an antibiotic to clear up the infection, then we'll try to ease her breathing with some steam.' She took a small bottle of medication out of a cupboard. Mandy handed her a syringe and Mrs Hope filled it with the antibiotic then gently injected it into the chinchilla.

'Good girl,' Mrs Hope soothed, massaging the chinchilla's skin where the needle had gone in. Then she crouched down in front of Beth. 'Stardust needs to stay in hospital for a few days,' she explained. 'It's just so that we can keep an eye on her. But don't worry. She'll soon be back to her old self again.'

When Mrs Wilson and Beth had left, Mandy took Stardust into the residential unit and settled her into a clean cage. Then she turned her attention to the other animals that had been admitted that day.

There was a young greyhound in an enclosure against the wall. He'd broken a bone in one front leg, and looked rather sorry for himself with his bulky white plaster cast. In another cage on an opposite shelf was a drowsy cat which was recovering from an operation to remove an infected tooth. The third patient was a guinea-pig that had gone off its food.

Mandy gave them all fresh water and removed the soiled newspaper from the greyhound's cage. The dog was pleased to see her and wagged his tail rapidly while Mandy stroked him. She smiled when he crossed his front legs in the way she'd seen other dogs of the breed doing so often. 'Even with that cast, you still look elegant,' she laughed.

She looked in on Stardust once more then went back to the reception room where Jean was bustling about, preparing to go home.

The grey-haired woman turned to Mandy. 'The weather must be really bad,' she said. 'My daughter has just rung to say she isn't going to bring the children over after all. It's a pity, but I suppose it's better that they stay where they are.'

Above the howling of the wind outside, there came the sound of an engine revving up.

'Oh, good! Simon's managed to start his van at last,' said Jean, picking up her umbrella and opening the door. 'He's giving me a lift home.' She glanced uneasily at the battered old vehicle in the car park outside. 'I just hope it keeps going. I don't fancy walking back in this weather.'

'I'm sure it'll be fine,' Mandy reassured her. 'Simon usually has to give the engine a bit of extra encouragement to start in cold weather. But once it gets going, it goes like a bomb!'

'As long as it doesn't explode like one,' chuckled Jean, going outside.

Mandy stood at the door and waved as the old

vehicle rattled down the driveway. When it was out of sight, she went back to the residential unit where her parents were giving the patients their last treatment of the day.

While Mr Hope gave the cat its medication, Mandy helped her mother with Stardust. They put a bowl of steaming water next to the cage then draped a thick towel over both bowl and cage so that Stardust could breathe in the steam.

Mrs Hope added a few drops of eucalyptus oil to the water. 'That should help to clear her airways,' she said. She glanced out of the window. The wind battered the trees in the garden while the rain poured down. 'Of course, this cold wet weather won't help very much,' she warned.

When all the animals had been seen to, the Hopes went into the cottage to prepare supper. They were just sitting down to eat when there was a loud grating noise above them.

'Oh no,' said Adam Hope. 'It sounds like we've lost that loose tile I've been meaning to fix.'

'Does that mean we'll get a leak?' asked Mrs Hope anxiously.

'Could do,' said Mr Hope glumly. 'The weather's too bad to go up on the roof at the moment. I'll have to check on it in the morning.'

After supper they went into the living room to watch the news. The top story was the bad weather that was sweeping across most of Yorkshire. There were already several reports of serious damage, with Walton being one of the worst-affected places so far. The Hopes watched closely as the screen showed wind-ravaged properties in and around the town.

'Hey!' Mandy exclaimed as a familiar building came on to the screen. 'That's my school!' A large tree had blown down, crashing into the building and smashing several windows. 'I'm sure those are the windows in the science laboratory,' she said. But before she had a chance to look more closely, the newscaster moved on to another story.

'I guess you'll find out all about it when you go back after Christmas,' said Mr Hope, getting up to put another log on the fire.

'I wonder if James saw it?' Mandy pondered.

'Phone him and find out,' suggested Mrs Hope.

Mandy went into the hall and dialled the Hunters' number.

'Did you see the news?' Mandy asked James as he answered the phone.

'No,' replied James. 'I've been in the loft, sorting out our Christmas decorations.'

Mandy told him what she'd just seen.

'Just as well it wasn't the classrooms,' James joked, 'or we'd have been in for a draughty time when school starts again!'

'I'm sure the storm will have cleared up before then,' Mandy said.

'It had better clear up before Christmas,' remarked James firmly. 'We haven't even got our tree yet, and Dad doesn't want to bring one back on the roof of the car in case the wind blows it off.'

'We haven't got one either,' Mandy said. As she spoke, the lamp on the table next to her dimmed slightly, then brightened up again. 'It looks like the wind's having a fine old time battering the electricity lines,' she observed. 'Our lights are flickering here.'

'Ours too,' said James. 'I guess I'd better not check the bulbs in our fairy lights tonight. I won't be able to tell if they're flashing properly or not!'

'I was going to check ours too—' Mandy began, but before she could finish her sentence, she was plunged into darkness . . .

Two

'Hey! We've had a power cut!' Mandy exclaimed.

'Us too,' answered James. 'I'd better help Mum and Dad find some candles.'

'Bye, James,' Mandy said. She hung up, then felt her way along the wall of the hall back to the living room. The soft orange glow of the fire spread a shadowy light around the room. Mandy could see her dad hunting about in the drawers beneath the TV unit. 'I'm sure there's a torch in here somewhere,' he said.

'I'll get some candles from the kitchen,' Mandy offered.

It was pitch black in there. Mandy couldn't see a thing in front of her. 'Ouch!' she muttered, knocking her funny bone against the corner of the dresser. She rubbed her elbow which tingled uncomfortably. *Why do they call it a funny bone when it isn't at all funny to bump it?* she wondered.

She groped around inside the dresser cupboard until she found a packet of candles and an old lantern. 'This'll do,' she said.

There was a box of matches on the dresser. Mandy struck one, then lit a candle and put it inside the lantern. The faint flickering light cast long-fingered shadows around the room.

'Here comes Florence Nightingale,' laughed Adam Hope when Mandy returned to the living room. He picked up some iron tongs and prodded the fire. There was a loud crackling and popping as orange sparks flew up the chimney.

'Isn't this cosy?' said Mr Hope, putting down the tongs and settling back into his chair.

'Mmm. But I hope it doesn't go on too long,' said his wife.

'I'm sure it won't,' Mr Hope said cheerfully. 'You'll probably find a tree has fallen on to some power lines and a repair team is already on its way.'

'I hope you're right,' said Mrs Hope. 'I was planning to catch up on some paperwork tonight. And I don't feel like doing it by candlelight.'

'Let's play cards by candlelight instead,' suggested Adam Hope.

'And toast some marshmallows on the fire,' Mandy added.

'Excellent idea!' grinned her dad.

Mandy fetched a bag of coconut-coated marshmallows and some long forks from the kitchen. Back in the living room, the three of them speared the marshmallows on to the ends of the forks then held them over the flames.

'Smells delicious!' declared Adam Hope, licking his lips as the aroma of toasted coconut wafted out from the fire. 'I'm almost glad we've got no electricity. We wouldn't have done this otherwise.'

They played cards and toasted marshmallows for the rest of the evening, all the while expecting the lights to come back on. But by ten-thirty, there was still no power.

Mrs Hope yawned and stood up. 'Time for bed, I think.'

'Yes. It's been a long day,' said Adam Hope,

standing up to stretch. He put the wrought-iron guard in front of the fire. 'And there's not much point sitting around waiting for the lights to come back on.'

They went upstairs, with Mandy carrying the lantern to light their way. She thought about the animals in the residential unit. The darkness wouldn't really bother them. But it was a good thing that Animal Ark had gas heating – especially since the chinchilla needed to be kept warm.

'Don't forget to blow out the candle before you go to sleep, Mandy,' said Mrs Hope at the top of the stairs.

'And make sure your bedside light is switched off, otherwise you'll be dazzled in the night if the electricity comes back on,' warned her dad.

But the power didn't come on during the night. And when Mandy woke early in the morning, the wind was still raging, and the rain was pelting hard against the windows.

She climbed out of bed and drew back the curtains. 'Look at that!' she exclaimed, startled at the sight that met her. 'What a mess!' Enormous puddles covered most of the garden, and fallen branches lay strewn all around. Mandy washed and dressed and was on her way downstairs when the phone rang.

She heard her dad answering it. 'I'll be there as soon as I can,' he said.

'What's happened, Dad?' Mandy asked, meeting him at the foot of the stairs.

'A cow's been badly hurt at Garland Farm,' said Adam Hope.

They went into the kitchen where Mrs Hope was putting a pot of water on the Aga range which the family used in winter. 'Just as well we've got this old stove,' she said. 'But all the same, the tea's going to take a bit longer than usual, I'm afraid.'

'I'll just have some orange juice for now,' said Adam Hope, pouring himself a glass from a jug on the table. 'But I expect I'll need a hot drink when I get back from Garland's.'

'How did the cow get hurt?' Mandy asked him.

'A barn collapsed and some heavy timbers fell on the poor creature,' her dad explained.

'Doesn't sound too good,' said Emily Hope, shaking her head sympathetically. 'Was it just one animal that was injured?'

'It seems to be,' said Mr Hope, gulping down the juice then picking up the car keys from the dresser. 'I'll just fetch my bag from the surgery, then I'll be on my way.'

'Be careful,' Emily Hope told him. 'That farm's really low-lying. There might be some flooding in that area.'

'I'll be all right in the Land-rover,' answered Mr Hope, taking a heavy waterproof jacket from a peg behind the door. 'I shouldn't be too long.'

Minutes later he was back in the kitchen, looking rather frustrated and very wet.

'What's the matter?' Mandy asked, through a mouthful of muesli.

'I can't get out of the garage,' Mr Hope explained. 'There's a massive branch lying just in front of it. I can't budge it on my own so I need some help to clear it out of the way.'

Mandy and Mrs Hope pulled on their wellington boots and raincoats and followed him outside. The wind whipped around them, tugging at their coats and driving stinging bursts of rain into their faces.

'It's much worse out here than I thought,' Mandy shouted above the roaring gale. She sloshed through puddles that were already ankle deep in places. Even the driveway was covered in water. 'I wonder what it's like in the lane?' she asked.

'Probably a lot like it is here,' said Mr Hope. 'But I'll find out – just as soon as I can get past this.' He kicked at the enormous branch that blocked the garage door.

'It's more a tree trunk than a branch,' said Mrs Hope. She wiped a wet strand of hair out of her eyes then looked up at a nearby oak tree. 'That's where it came from,' she said, pointing to a ragged gash half-way up the trunk. 'We're lucky it didn't fall on the roof.'

'Just shows how strong this gale is if it can break something this big,' said Mr Hope. He bent down and slid his hands under one end of the log. 'You two take the other end.'

With much heaving and straining, they finally managed to shift the heavy branch to one side. Mr Hope drove away, the wheels of the Land-rover shooting huge sprays of water to either side.

Mrs Hope and Mandy watched him go before paddling round to the surgery. 'Let's check on the animals and brace ourselves for whatever else the day has in store for us!' remarked Mrs Hope.

'You mean more rain?' Mandy frowned, looking up at the heavy skies.

'It certainly looks like it,' said her mother.

They pulled off their wellies and went inside. Already, the phone was ringing again.

Mandy answered it. It was Mrs Ponsonby. 'I don't want to take Pandora and Toby out in such atrocious conditions,' she boomed. Pandora was a spoilt Pekinese and Toby was a mongrel puppy. 'So they won't be in for their check-up today. I'll make another appointment when this ghastly rain and wind have stopped.'

Mrs Ponsonby wasn't the only person to cancel her appointment. Minutes later, another pet owner rang up to say she'd rather not come out in the bad weather.

Two more phone calls followed in quick succession. First, Jean Knox rang to say she couldn't get in because a mudslide had blocked her road. 'The council says they're so busy dealing with emergencies, they won't be able to clear it up until tomorrow,' she said, sounding flustered.

Then Simon called to say that his van wouldn't start. 'I think the engine must have got waterlogged when I was driving home last night,' he told Mandy.

'I'm amazed to hear you even made it home

after the way it was spluttering yesterday,' Mandy teased.

'There's nothing wrong with my van,' said Simon defensively. 'It just doesn't like water.'

'You mean it doesn't like *working*,' Mandy joked, before hanging up.

Mrs Hope studied the remaining appointments in the diary. 'You know, none of these cases is particularly urgent,' she said to Mandy, 'so I think we should cancel them all. I'm sure most people won't relish coming out today.'

They contacted the pet owners, who were very happy to bring their animals in a day or two later. Then Emily Hope rang the electricity department to find out when they could expect the power to come back on. 'Not for several more days!' she echoed with astonishment upon hearing the reply.

She hung up, shaking her head. 'Apparently the gale brought down a pylon and some major power lines,' she explained to Mandy. 'And it's a huge job to sort it all out. So we're stuck with candles and fires for the time being.'

Mandy shrugged. 'I'm getting quite used to not switching on the lights,' she said, following her mum into the residential unit.

The greyhound must have heard them before they came in because he was waiting at the gate to his cage, his slim body trembling with excitement.

'Hello, Marco,' said Mrs Hope, opening the gate and checking his leg. 'I think you can go home today – if your owner can make it here to fetch you!'

'And how are you today, Stardust?' Mandy asked, going over to the chinchilla.

Stardust looked just as miserable as before. She hadn't touched her food and was still having trouble breathing. She wheezed noisily, in short, shallow breaths. 'I don't think *you're* ready to go home,' Mandy said.

Mrs Hope joined Mandy next to the cage. 'I'll give her another injection in a minute. In the meantime, you can give her the steam and eucalyptus treatment again. I'll go and switch the kettle on to boil some . . .' She stopped. 'Oh no! I forgot,' she grumbled. 'No electricity!'

'I'll fetch some hot water from the kitchen,' Mandy offered. 'It's lucky you put that pan on the Aga at breakfast time.' She fetched the water and set up Stardust's steam treatment.

Mrs Hope was examining the cat and the guinea-pig. When she'd seen to them, she came over to Mandy. 'They're much better,' she said. 'I'd like them to go home, like Marco. We'll ring their owners to let them know.'

But only the cat's owner said he'd come round immediately. Marco and the guinea-pig's owners were reluctant to come out just then. They asked if they could wait until later in the day to see if the weather improved.

'Never mind,' Mandy said, stroking the guinea-pig who was now hungrily munching up her food. 'We'll take good care of you here.'

'Still, I'm sure they'll be happier in their own surroundings,' said Mrs Hope. 'Perhaps Dad will be able to take them home when he comes back.'

'After he's had his hot drink,' Mandy reminded her mum with a smile.

The cat's owner arrived within twenty minutes. 'Just as well I drive a jeep,' he said. 'Most of the roads are several centimetres under water. If it carries on raining like this, the river might burst its banks, and then we could be in for some serious flooding.' He draped a plastic sheet over the cat's basket then dashed outside and drove away, churning up a wake on the driveway behind him.

By the time Adam Hope came home later that morning, the garden was even more waterlogged. The huge puddles on the lawn were growing by the minute. A lot of them had even joined up to form bigger ones. Mandy watched the Land-rover splashing through the water as it came up the drive. *It looks as though Dad's driving through a river*, she thought to herself.

She pulled on her wellies again and waded out to meet him. 'Is the cow all right?' she asked, entering the garage.

'She will be,' Mr Hope replied, climbing out of the Land-rover. 'She's badly cut and bruised, so she's in a lot of pain. But luckily nothing was broken. I said I'd check on her again tomorrow.' He looked out at the teeming rain. 'I just hope I'll be able to make it there,' he said grimly. 'It's pretty heavy going right now and it's worsening by the minute.'

Mandy took a deep breath. 'Would you mind risking one more trip today?' she asked her dad.

Mr Hope looked at her aghast. 'You mean go out in this weather again?'

'Uh-huh,' Mandy nodded. 'You see we need

to take Marco and the guinea-pig home,' she explained. 'Their owners are worried about coming out.'

'And what about poor me having to risk life and limb again?' grinned Mr Hope.

'But you've got a Land-rover, and it won't take long, Dad,' Mandy said. 'They live quite close to each other. And I'll help you.'

Adam Hope jangled his keys. 'Well, if we're to make it back home again before the lane's completely flooded, we'd better get a move on.'

Mandy ran back to the residential unit. She put the guinea-pig in a basket then took Marco out of his cage. 'Sorry, Stardust,' she said, glancing across to the chinchilla's cage. 'It won't be long before you can go home too.'

Mr Hope came in and picked up the guinea-pig's basket. 'Ready?' he asked Mandy.

Mandy nodded. She tucked Marco inside her jacket to keep him dry, then followed her father back out to the garage.

'The animals went in two-by-two,' Mr Hope recited with a grin as he slid the guinea-pig's basket on to the back seat of the Land-rover.

'But not as *odd* pairs of animals, Dad,' laughed

Mandy. She climbed into the passenger seat then opened her jacket. Marco's long slender nose peeped out. He craned his arched neck and stared quizzically out of the window.

'Ready to set sail, Marco?' Mandy chuckled as Mr Hope reversed out of the garage then turned the Land-rover and set off for the village. As they passed under the Animal Ark sign, Mandy saw at once why her dad was worried about the lane. It was already several inches under water.

'I'm not sure this is wise,' said Mr Hope, steering carefully through the flood. But he pressed on and soon they were on higher ground, heading for the housing estate on the other side of the village.

They delivered the animals to their grateful owners then turned for home. It was lunchtime as they came to the Fox and Goose, the pub in the centre of Welford. Usually people would be arriving for a meal now. But, today, there wasn't anybody about. And, even worse, the Christmas lights which festooned the low stone building no longer lent the place a cheerful air. Instead, they clung damply to the eaves, their bulbs extinguished and water dripping constantly from them.

'It's so gloomy!' Mandy groaned.

The tall Christmas tree in front of the pub was surrounded by an enormous puddle. Someone had tied a thick rope to the trunk of the tree and secured it to a post nearby.

'I suppose that's to stop it being blown down or washed away,' said Mr Hope.

'The poor thing looks almost sad,' Mandy commented. The tree's branches, heavy with water, sagged limply towards the ground, twitching in the wind. And on the top the silver star hung down, crumpled and battered out of shape.

'It's not at all like Christmas,' Mandy murmured. 'If only this horrid weather would clear up.'

'Not much chance of that for a day or two,' said her dad, turning into the lane. The drains on both sides of the narrow road had become blocked and were spewing rubbish and more water out into the lane. 'But just think how terrific it will be when it eventually *does* stop raining and all of this clears up,' Mr Hope added, gesturing ahead of him.

The Land-rover bumped along, its wheels churning up the puddles into a muddy brown froth. At last, they came to Animal Ark.

'Home sweet home,' Mandy grinned. But as

they started up the driveway, she gasped. The cottage was almost completely surrounded by water. 'It's like an island!' she said.

Mr Hope drove into the garage. Water was beginning to seep in under the door so that Mandy and her dad stepped down from the Land-rover into a pool on the floor.

Mr Hope looked troubled. 'This is getting serious,' he said. 'The river must have burst its banks, and flooded all the way up here. We're going to have to stop the water from coming in.' He looked around the garage. A row of bulky bags stood against the back wall. 'Those sacks of compost might do the trick.'

'You mean, use them like sandbags?' Mandy asked.

'Uh-huh,' nodded her dad. 'We'll stack them up outside the door.' Working fast, they lined the bags up in front of the garage door. Every time she stooped to wedge another bag into place, Mandy felt raindrops seeping down her neck.

'Not quite as good as sand,' said Mr Hope. 'But it's all we have.'

By the time they had finished, they were both drenched. They ran through the teeming rain to the front porch where Mrs Hope was waiting for them. 'You're just in the nick of time,' she told them as they went indoors. 'I've heard on the radio that the river has burst its banks upstream. The weather office has put out a severe flood warning for Welford.'

'We're going to be marooned,' said Mandy.

'Probably,' said Mrs Hope. 'Let's just hope that the house doesn't get flooded.'

Mr Hope nodded gravely. Then a smile spread across his face. 'At least we're in an ark,' he said. His joke lightened the gloomy atmosphere.

'Let's hope it's a waterproof ark,' smiled Mrs Hope.

'Not if Dad's roof repairs are anything to go by,' Mandy said, looking up to the ceiling where a damp patch had formed.

Her father grimaced. 'It never rains but it pours,' he said with a sigh. He thought for a second. 'I guess I'd better have a go at fixing that now before it develops into a major problem.'

'Good idea, Noah,' chuckled Mrs Hope. 'And while you're up there, Mandy and I will see to Stardust again.'

Alone in the residential unit, the chinchilla looked more dejected than ever. But just when Mandy was wondering if the little animal was ever going to get better, Stardust hopped over to her food bowl and began nibbling on one of the pellets.

'Good girl,' Mandy said encouragingly. She turned to her mum. 'Shouldn't we take her into the cottage with us? She's very lonely in here.'

Mrs Hope smiled at Mandy and shook her head in amusement. 'Mandy Hope. The vet-to-be with a heart of gold!'

'We can keep her in the living room in her cage so we don't have to keep coming in here to check on her,' Mandy said persuasively.

Emily Hope shrugged her shoulders. 'Well, I don't see the harm in it. And you're right. Since she's our only patient, we might as well have her in the cottage.'

They put Stardust in a portable cage and carried her into the living room. The chinchilla looked around her new surroundings with interest then began nibbling her food again.

*   *   *

After lunch, James phoned up. 'Are you floating yet?' he asked Mandy.

'Nearly,' she replied, gazing out of the hall window at the rising flood water. And then she saw something else – something bright red bobbing about outside.

'Hey! What's that?' she said, standing up and leaning towards the window for a better look.

'What's what?' came James's confused voice.

'It's a little boat!' Mandy exclaimed.

'A toy one?' asked James.

'No. It's real. And hang on, there's another . . . and another! Just a minute, James.' She dropped the receiver on to the table and ran over to the door.

Behind her, James's puzzled voice called down the line, 'Mandy! What's going on? Where are you?'

Mandy opened the front door. An amazing sight greeted her. Animal Ark was besieged by a flotilla of small rowing boats! Unmanned, they bobbed about on the water, their oars stowed neatly in their shafts.

'Mandy!' called out James again. 'What's happened?'

Mandy turned and picked up the phone. 'You won't believe this, James,' she said. 'But Animal Ark has just become a harbour!'

Three

'James reckons they're from that boat-hire company on the river,' Mandy told her mum and dad after ringing off from James and calling them to see the boats.

'That makes sense,' agreed Mrs Hope. 'The gale must have made them break their moorings. Then they floated down here when the river flooded.'

'We'd better let the hire company know where they are,' said Mr Hope, flipping through the telephone directory to find the number.

The owner, Andrew Bond, was hugely relieved to find out where his boats were. He said he'd arrange to have them collected as soon as the floods subsided.

'That might not be for days,' Mandy said to her mum and dad, staring out at the driving rain. 'What if they float off somewhere else in the meantime?'

'I don't think that'll happen,' said Mr Hope. 'They're already clustering together at the side of the garage. It looks like the current comes to a stop there so it's a sort of natural mooring.'

Except for one boat which was firmly jammed against the front steps, all the boats gradually converged next to the garage. Drifting along on the tide, they edged closer together, bumping and jostling one another, their bright colours looking almost festive on the grey water. *Just as well I've finished all my shopping*, Mandy thought. With only five days to go before Christmas, and the flood water rising, she might not have had another chance to do it.

She spent the rest of the afternoon half-heartedly sorting through decorations and hanging tinsel around the fireplace. There was an artificial Christmas tree in the loft and Mandy hauled it down to the living room. 'Not as nice as a real one but I suppose it's better than nothing,' she said to her parents. 'Of course, some fairy lights would help!' she sighed, fed up that the power was still off.

From her cage nearby, Stardust stared out at the tree.

'Do you want to have a closer look?' Mandy said to the chinchilla. She gently lifted her out of the cage and carried her over to the tree.

Stardust sniffed at the lower branches, but she quickly lost interest in the artificial leaves and hopped away to investigate a plant. She started to nibble at a leaf then stopped and twitched her nose before making a bee-line for a bowl of hazelnuts on the hearth.

'Hey! Those are mine!' said Adam Hope, scooping up the dish just as Stardust dipped her head into it.

The chinchilla sat back, a look of disappointment on her fluffy face.

'Don't be mean, Dad,' laughed Mandy. 'It's Christmas, remember? The season of goodwill. You should be sharing.'

Mr Hope gave her a lopsided grin. 'I'll remember that the next time I see you tucking into something delicious!' He reached down and gave Stardust a hazelnut. The chinchilla quickly munched it up then looked up at him, hoping for another.

'She's so much better,' said Mrs Hope. 'It's a shame we're cut off like this – she could have gone home this afternoon.'

Mandy picked up Stardust and cuddled her velvety soft body. 'I'm not sorry you're stuck with us,' she whispered. 'You're really sweet and it will be fun to have you around for a few more days.'

'Just as well she's our only patient,' said Mr Hope, putting the nuts on the mantelpiece, well out of Stardust's reach. 'Otherwise you'd have had me sharing my meals with all and sundry!'

'No danger of that for a day or two,' said Mrs Hope. 'I can't imagine anyone even trying to bring an animal to us now.'

'But what if there's an emergency?' Mandy asked, suddenly feeling worried. She carried Stardust back to her cage and put her inside.

'Let's not worry about things that haven't happened,' said Mr Hope.

'But what *would* you do if an animal fell seriously ill?' Mandy persisted, flopping down on the sofa.

Mr Hope looked thoughtful for a moment. He smoothed his beard with one hand then said, 'We'd make a plan, but don't ask me now what it would be. We'll just have to cross that bridge when – and if – the time comes.'

Mandy's worst fears were realised the very next day when the phone rang during breakfast.

Emily Hope went into the hall then came back a minute later. 'It's Walter Pickard,' she said. 'He's worried about Scraps. She's gone off her food.'

Walter Pickard was a retired butcher who lived in a cottage behind the Fox and Goose. He had three cats, Scraps and Missie, who were both ginger and rather old, and Tom, a black and white tomcat.

'That's unusual for Scraps,' Mandy commented. 'She normally eats anything.'

'Are there any other symptoms?' asked Mr Hope.

'Walter said she's very lethargic and that she's been soiling her basket lately,' said Emily Hope. 'It doesn't sound too good. I explained to Walter that we're cut off, but said we'd try to arrange something.' She looked anxiously out of the kitchen window at the flood water. 'But what?'

'I'll contact Steve Wimberley from the practice in Walton and see if he can get through to him,' said Adam Hope. 'I was going to ask if he could see to the Garland's cow anyway, seeing as I can't get to the farm now.'

Mr Hope contacted the Walton vet who said he could make it to Garland Farm because it was on the other side of the river from Welford. But the road into the village was completely underwater so he wouldn't be able to get to Walter.

'That just means we have to come up with another plan, Dad,' Mandy said in a matter-of-fact voice. Scraps simply *had* to get the treatment she needed. Mandy never gave up on a sick animal, no matter how difficult the circumstances were. 'Even if we have to *walk* there!' she added earnestly.

'It's more likely we'll have to *swim*,' her dad pointed out, going over to the window. 'That water out there's not just knee-deep any more.'

'There's got to be a way of getting through,' said Mandy, her mind searching for an idea. And then it came to her. 'The boats!' she exclaimed. 'That's the answer. We can *row* to Walter's!'

Mr Hope clicked his fingers. 'Good thinking, Mandy,' he declared. 'And luckily there's one still wedged up against the front steps. We shouldn't even have to get our feet wet!'

They rang the hire company to ask if they could borrow the boat. The owner was very happy to oblige. 'Glad to be of some service in a crisis,' he said.

Within minutes, Mandy and her dad were ready to go. They went out to the porch and Mr Hope reached for the boat that was still wedged against the steps. 'I'll hold it steady while you get in,' he told Mandy.

Gingerly, Mandy climbed into the boat. It wobbled violently and she had to grab the sides to stop herself from falling out. 'Phew!' she breathed, sitting down quickly.

Mr Hope handed her his bulky vet's bag then tried to get in with her. But before he had both feet in the boat, it began to drift away from the steps. 'Oops!' he exclaimed, swaying and teetering on his back foot as the gulf between the boat and the step widened.

But just when it seemed that Mr Hope would be pulled into the water, he heaved himself forward. 'Hold tight!' he cried, sitting down heavily next to Mandy. The little boat lurched under his weight and for a second Mandy thought it would capsize.

'Sorry about that, love,' said Mr Hope when the rocking subsided. 'But I had to make a leap for it!'

Mandy laughed. 'I wish I'd had a camera with me.'

'I'm glad you didn't,' smiled Mr Hope, picking up the oars and handing one to Mandy.

They struck out across the flooded garden then paddled under the Animal Ark sign. Mandy gasped when she saw that the lane had completely disappeared beneath the flood water. 'It's like a river!' she said.

'It *is* a river,' responded her dad. 'Now that the original one has burst its banks.'

The wind had eased but it was still strong enough to buffet the boat and whip up icy sprays of water which showered Mandy and her dad as they rowed along.

'The flood's washed down all sorts of things,' Mandy remarked, pointing to a tyre and a half-submerged plastic bucket that were being swept along in the swirling water ahead of them.

'Keep a look out for heavy things like uprooted trees,' said Mr Hope, deftly manoeuvring the boat past a thick branch that was rushing along next to them.

The swiftly flowing water helped to propel them onward so it wasn't long before they reached the crossroads in the centre of Welford. Like the previous day, there was little life in the village. And today, the Fox and Goose looked even more drab and uninviting. The car park was swamped, and muddy water lapped over the edge of the front porch.

Mandy and Adam Hope pulled on their oars, navigating the boat down the side of the pub to Walter's little cottage. They dragged the boat on to the top step then knocked on the battered front door.

'Thank goodness you managed to find a way to get here,' said Walter when he opened the door and saw the boat. He led them into his tiny living-room. Scraps was lying very still on a cushion near the fire. A bowl of cat biscuits and pieces of chicken sat beside her. Scraps opened her eyes when Mr Hope bent down in front of her but closed them again immediately. Mandy realised with a sinking feeling that the sick cat didn't have the energy to keep them open.

Mr Hope gently examined Scraps. He listened to her heart and lungs then felt her belly before finally taking a urine sample. While Mr Hope tested the sample, Walter and Mandy looked on apprehensively, hoping for news that would mean Scraps would soon be well again.

But Mr Hope could offer little comfort. 'I'm afraid things aren't looking too good for Scraps,' he said softly. 'I'm pretty certain her kidneys are failing. It's a common disease in ageing cats,' he told Walter. He took a syringe out of his bag and filled it with some medication. 'I'll give her a vitamin B injection to help deal with the build-up of toxins, but the main thing now is to keep her as comfortable as possible. And try to get her to drink, Walter. If she doesn't, I'll have to put her on a drip.'

'Oh, she's drinking quite a bit of water,' said Walter, his voice a mixture of hope and anxiety. 'That's a good sign, isn't it?'

Mr Hope smiled sympathetically but said nothing. He carefully injected Scraps then put the used needle into a disposal bag. Closing his vet's bag, he said, 'With a little encouragement, Scraps may start eating again, but I'm afraid I can't promise a dramatic improvement. After all, she is in her twilight years now.' He put a hand on Walter's shoulder and said kindly, 'I'm sorry, Walter.'

The old man swallowed hard and turned away. He knelt down next to Scraps and stroked her lightly. 'Poor old girl,' he murmured, his gentle voice breaking with emotion.

Mandy felt a lump forming in her throat. The last time she'd seen Scraps, she'd been sneaking a biscuit off the table in Walter's kitchen. And now she was lying so still, not showing the slightest interest in food. Mandy crouched down and kissed the top of the old cat's head. 'I'll come and see you again soon, Scraps,' she said.

As Mandy and Mr Hope turned to go, Tom, the black and white cat, came into the room. He was an unfriendly animal who usually ignored Walter's visitors. But, today, Mandy thought he seemed different. He walked over to Scraps and sniffed her. Then he sat next to her and gently licked the sick cat's ears.

'It looks like he's trying to comfort Scraps,' Mandy said with surprise.

'Aye. He's been fussing about her since yesterday,' said Walter. 'I've never seen him doing anything like it.'

'He must know that Scraps is ill. It just shows how little we understand of cats,' said Mr Hope. He opened the front door and said to Walter, 'I'll check on Scraps again in the morning. But if you need me before then, I'll come round right away.'

'Thanks, Adam,' said Walter hoarsely. 'I know you're doing everything you can.'

Mandy and Mr Hope climbed back into the boat. In silence, they paddled round to the front of the pub. They were halfway across the flooded green when Mandy spotted James in a small rubber dinghy. He was on the opposite side of the green, paddling strongly towards them.

'I wonder what he's up to?' Mandy mused.

James rowed over to them, the dinghy bouncing lightly over the choppy water.

'I've been fetching supplies for some of our neighbours,' he said, pointing to a box of groceries in front of him. 'Luckily Mrs McFarlane still had some bread and milk in stock.'

Mrs McFarlane ran the local post office. It was the only shop in the village so she sold all sorts of things, including groceries.

'We've been on an urgent mission too,' Mandy said. She told James about Scraps. 'She's really very ill,' she finished.

'Poor old cat,' said James. 'And poor Walter. He'll be broken-hearted if anything happens to Scraps.'

'Unfortunately that's all part of giving your

heart to an animal,' said Adam Hope. 'Pets give us lots of joy but sooner or later we're in for heartache with them. And even though we may be prepared for it to happen, it's always a big wrench when it does.'

That night, Mandy lay in bed thinking of Walter and Scraps. She wondered just how much longer the two old friends had together. She hoped that Scraps was feeling a little better after the injection, and that she'd been able to eat something, even if it was only a temporary improvement.

She sighed. Her dad was right. With the joy of owning a pet came the sadness of parting with it. And even though Walter had two other cats which he adored, it would still be very hard for him if Scraps didn't make it.

She was about to blow out the candle in the lantern when she became aware of an odd bumping sound. It was coming from downstairs.

Stardust? Mandy wondered at once, remembering another chinchilla called Peanut which had got loose in Animal Ark and taken up residence in the chimney. *Surely she hasn't escaped from her cage? I thought I closed it properly.*

She pulled on her dressing gown then picked up the lantern and went downstairs. The bumping continued rhythmically. *It's not coming from in here after all*, Mandy decided, going into the living room.

All the same, she thought it best to check on Stardust. She went over to the cage. The gate was firmly closed and Stardust was fast asleep, tightly curled into a fluffy grey ball.

Mandy was puzzled. *So what* is *making that noise?* she thought.

She listened again and decided that the noise was coming from outside, near the front door. *It's probably the rowing boat knocking against the porch. I'll have to stop it, otherwise it'll keep me awake all night*, she decided.

Her wellies were standing next to the door in the hall. She pulled them on, expecting to slosh about in the water on the steps as she tried to grab the boat. But when she opened the door and stepped out on to the porch, she saw that the boat was quite still, its prow lodged securely on the top step.

Perplexed, Mandy looked around. The strange noise was coming from somewhere to her right.

She lifted the lantern higher, trying to see what was there.

And then, in the soft glow given off by the candle, she noticed a rounded object bumping against the cottage wall. Intrigued, she leaned out over the edge of the porch to get a closer look.

'Oh! It's only an old barrel,' she said to herself, recognising the shape. 'Just more flotsam washed down by the floods.' The wooden tub was bobbing upright in the water with its top end open.

She reached out to push the barrel away from the house but, as her hand caught hold of it, she saw a small movement inside.

And then she heard a faint sound.

'There's something in there!' Mandy exclaimed.

Quickly she pulled the barrel towards her. As it came into the candlelight she saw a pair of bright eyes staring up at her.

'It's a cat!' Mandy cried.

Four

'Oh, you poor thing,' Mandy breathed, reaching into the barrel with her free hand. She grasped the loose skin at the back of the cat's neck. In one smooth movement, she hauled the sodden little creature out and held it securely against her waist.

The barrel bobbed and lurched before being caught up once more in the current.

'Just in time,' Mandy said, as it drifted into the watery darkness. Beneath her arm, the cat trembled and shivered. 'Is that because you're cold, or afraid, or both?' Mandy said softly, looking down at the soggy little creature. It was black and white with big, staring green eyes.

Quickly Mandy went inside. She put the lantern on the table in the hall and prised off her boots with one hand while holding the cat in the other. Then, picking up the lantern again, she went into the kitchen.

There she found a clean, dry towel which she wrapped around the cat. 'We'll go next to the Aga where it's nice and warm,' she said, pulling a chair over to the cooker. She sat down and, holding the cat in her lap, gently towelled it dry.

'There. That's better,' Mandy said, unwrapping the towel after a few minutes. The cat's fur no longer clung damply to its skin. 'Now what's a pretty girl like you doing out on those floods?'

The cat was still shivering uncontrollably. She sat hunched in Mandy's lap and stared rigidly at a point somewhere ahead of her.

'Perhaps you're hungry,' Mandy wondered. Carefully, she eased the cat off her lap and put her on to another chair. Then she poured some milk into a saucer and held it in front of the tense little animal.

But the frightened cat showed no interest in the milk.

'I guess you're too shocked to want anything,' Mandy said. 'I just hope you're not hurt or ill.' She looked at the kitchen clock. The luminous hands showed that it was nearly midnight. 'It's ages to go before morning,' she said. 'I wish Mum or Dad would wake up.'

Mandy picked up the cat again and cuddled her closely, trying to help her relax. 'You still feel so cold. And I really don't like the way you're trembling.'

The cat fixed her bright green eyes on Mandy's face and stared at her pitifully.

Mandy made up her mind in an instant. 'You can't wait till morning,' she said decisively. 'I'm going to wake Mum and Dad. They'll understand when they see what a state you're in.'

But as she opened the door, she nearly collided with her mother who was coming into the kitchen at that same moment.

'I thought I heard something down here,' said Emily Hope. Then she saw the cat in Mandy's arms. 'And who is this?'

'An unexpected visitor, you could say,' Mandy

said. She quickly explained how she'd found the cat.

'Poor little creature,' said Mrs Hope. 'She must have been terrified. I'd better have a good look at her.' She took the cat from Mandy and carried her over to the kitchen table. 'Can you put a towel on the table and light a few more candles for me, Mandy?' she asked.

Mandy found another dry towel and spread it out on to the table. Then she fetched the candles from the living room and arranged them around the kitchen. They lent the room a warm, almost cheerful air. Mandy thought that in different circumstances, it would have looked quite festive.

'Would you bring me the emergency bag please, Mandy?' asked Mrs Hope. 'Dad left it in the hall this morning when you came back from Walter's.'

Mandy fetched the bag and Mrs Hope began by checking the cat's temperature. 'Mmm. A little on the cold side, but that's hardly surprising,' Mrs Hope murmured. She took out a stethoscope and listened to the animal's heartbeat and breathing. 'That's all fine,' she said, before examining the cat for signs of injury. Finally, with the help of a small torch, she checked her eyes and ears. At last

Mrs Hope looked across at Mandy and said, 'Well, apart from being cold and in shock, she's absolutely fine. All she needs is to be kept warm and quiet for a few days.'

'That's easy,' Mandy said, relieved that the cat's watery adventure had caused her no real harm. 'And I think she ought to stay with me for the rest of the night.'

'Just tonight,' agreed Mrs Hope, blowing out the candles. 'Then tomorrow we'll put her – and Stardust – in the residential unit. Otherwise the cottage will really start to resemble an ark, especially if we have any more animals arriving unexpectedly!'

Cradling the cat in her arms, Mandy carried her upstairs. Mrs Hope followed behind, lighting the way with the lantern.

'Let's give her a name,' Mandy suggested. 'Even if it's just a temporary one.' She was sure the cat's owners would soon be looking for her, and then they'd find out what her real name was. But in the meantime, it would be nice to call her something.

'Any suggestions?' asked Mrs Hope, waiting with the lantern so that Mandy could see her way across to her bed.

Mandy studied the cat for a second. The candlelight danced against the little animal's black and white coat, highlighting now and again her white chest and her bright green eyes. The hazy, leaping glow triggered Mandy's imagination. 'What about Flicker?' she said.

'That suits her perfectly,' agreed her mum.

Mandy lay the cat on her bed. 'So, little watery cat. We'll call you Flicker. I hope you like your new name.' She slipped under her duvet and curled herself around the warm cat's body.

'She ought to feel quite safe and cosy now,' smiled Mrs Hope. She turned to go. 'Sleep well, both of you.'

Darkness flooded Mandy's room as Mrs Hope went out, taking the lantern with her. Soon, Mandy couldn't even see her hand in front of her as she gently smoothed Flicker.

In the blackness of the night, the silence in the old house seemed even deeper. But suddenly the quiet was broken by a mournful miaow.

'It's all right, Flicker,' crooned Mandy, drawing the cat closer to her.

But Flicker could not be consoled. She miaowed again, this time more woefully.

'You're safe,' Mandy said in a calm, reassuring voice. But she could tell that Flicker didn't feel at all safe. Against her chest, Mandy could feel the cat's heart beating rapidly. 'What's the matter, Flicker? Is there something there?' Mandy asked. Perhaps, being able to see in the dark, the cat had spotted something that had frightened her. After all, she'd just been through a horrible ordeal, so anything strange would be sure to upset her.

Mandy sat up and felt in her bedside drawer for the torch she always kept there. All the while, Flicker kept up her pitiful mewing.

Finding the torch, Mandy switched it on and flashed it around the room. At the same time, Flicker stopped miaowing.

'See. Nothing scary in here,' Mandy said, switching off the torch and lying down again.

Flicker responded with another pitiful cry.

'I promise you there's nothing to be frightened of,' Mandy sighed, reaching for the torch once more. 'But let's have one more look to make sure.'

Again, Flicker's cries stopped when Mandy shone the beam around the room.

Suddenly Mandy realised what the problem was. 'Poor little Flicker. You don't like the dark!' she breathed. 'I guess it reminds you of what it was like in that barrel. Well, Mum's got the lantern and we can't leave the torch on all night because we need to save the batteries. But don't worry, I'll sort out something else for you.'

She slid out of bed and made her way down to the kitchen. *I'm getting pretty good at this*, she thought to herself with a smile as she felt around in the dark for one of the candles that had been burning just a short while ago. She found

one on the worktop then ran her hand along the window sill until she came across the box of matches she'd left there earlier.

Mandy lit the candle then took an empty glass jar out of a cupboard. 'This should do the trick,' she said, letting some wax drip into the bottom of the jar. Carefully, she pushed the candle into the molten wax then hurried back upstairs.

'Look what I've made for you, Flicker,' she whispered as she tiptoed into her bedroom. She put the jar on the bedside table. 'It's a night light.'

Mandy switched off the torch which she'd left on for Flicker while she was downstairs, then slid under her warm duvet. The makeshift night light gave off a comforting glow. 'What do you think of that, Flicker?' Mandy asked quietly.

The timid cat looked at Mandy, her eyes reflecting the soft yellow candlelight. She blinked then opened her mouth in a wide yawn.

'You're exhausted,' Mandy said, smoothing Flicker's silky coat. 'It's been a long, frightening night for you, hasn't it?'

Flicker blinked again, this time very slowly as if her eyelids had grown heavy and she was battling to keep them open. She forced her eyes open

again, but only for a moment before she gave in
and allowed them to close. And then, at last, to
Mandy's delight, Flicker curled herself up into a
tight little ball and fell asleep.

Five

A solid blob of wax at the bottom of the jar was all that was left of the night light when Mandy woke up in the morning. Flicker was still curled up against her, fast asleep. *Just as well she didn't wake up when the candle burnt down*, Mandy thought. *I might have had to make another night light in a hurry.*

As she inched herself out of bed, she tried not to disturb the cat. But Flicker seemed to feel her moving and woke with a start. She shook her head then stared at Mandy with a startled look on her face.

'It's all right,' Mandy said, putting out her hand to stroke Flicker. 'It's me, remember? The one who rescued you from the water.'

Flicker shrank back from Mandy's hand and sat huddled up, watching her suspiciously.

'You're really timid, aren't you?' Mandy murmured, moving slowly away from Flicker. 'Don't worry, I'll leave you alone for a while. I'm sure you'll soon get used to me.'

She dressed then closed her bedroom door before going downstairs. Flicker had had one lucky escape already. But she might not be so fortunate if she slipped out of the house and ended up in the flood water again.

'How's Flicker this morning?' asked Mrs Hope, meeting Mandy at the bottom of the stairs.

'Awake but very nervous,' Mandy answered. 'So I don't think we should move her to the residential unit yet.'

Mrs Hope nodded. 'You're probably right. We'll give her time to settle down first.'

Mandy collected a litter tray and some food for Flicker then went back upstairs to her bedroom.

Flicker was sitting on the table under the window, looking down at the flooded garden. As soon as she heard the door open, she leaped to the ground and hid under the table.

'It's only me,' Mandy said quietly as she put the litter box on the floor near the door.

Flicker looked out at her from under the table, her eyes wide with distrust.

'And I've brought you some breakfast,' Mandy went on, crouching down and carefully sliding the dish towards the cat.

Flicker eyed the food but made no move towards it.

'I bet you're starving,' Mandy said. 'But you're not going to eat until I leave, are you?' She straightened up then left Flicker alone again and went to see to Stardust.

She was washing out the chinchilla's water dish when Mr Hope came into the kitchen. 'Want to come with me to check on Scraps?' he asked her. 'I could do with some help rowing.'

'OK,' Mandy said, pleased to be able to visit her old friend again so soon.

'I'm going to try to get to Garland's Farm as well,' said Mr Hope. 'Ivor Garland rang to say that Mr Wimberley won't be able to check on the heifer today because there's an emergency on another farm. A flock of sheep is marooned in the fells. But the cow still needs treatment.'

'No wonder you need a rowing companion,' smiled Mandy.

They were preparing to leave when James rang up. 'It's really boring for Blackie, being cooped up indoors like this,' he told Mandy. 'He's driving us all crazy.'

Blackie was James's very lively black Labrador. Mandy knew just how frustrated he would be at having to stay inside for so long. Blackie had so much energy that even after a long walk, he still had plenty of bounce left in him. 'Why don't you let him go out for a swim?' she joked.

'I have. By accident!' groaned James. 'When I came in with the shopping yesterday, he slipped out of the door. Next thing I knew, he was paddling down the road!'

Mandy could picture the scene – Blackie swimming madly away and James yelling at him to come back. 'How did you get him to come home?' she asked curiously. Blackie was well known for ignoring James when he called him.

'I had to go after him in my dinghy and lure him back with some dog biscuits!' James explained. 'He was grinning from ear to ear by the time we got home! I think he thought it was all a big game. But he wasn't too happy when Mum made him stay on the porch until he was dry.'

'We had a soggy animal in our house last night too,' Mandy said. She told James about Flicker. 'No one's rung up about a missing cat so far,' she continued. 'So it looks like we might have to start looking for her owner.'

'That won't exactly be easy right now,' said James. 'But I tell you what. I'm taking the dinghy to fetch some more things from the post office this morning. If I tell Mrs McFarlane about Flicker, she can tell everyone she sees.'

'Good idea,' Mandy said. 'And we might even bump into you again. Dad and I are going out in the boat in a minute to see Scraps.'

The journey to Walter's cottage was easier now that the wind was just a light breeze and the rain was beginning to let up. But the flood water was still very high, submerging all the roads in and around the village. The only way to get anywhere without getting wet was definitely still by boat.

When Mandy and her dad arrived at the

cottage, they found Scraps lying exactly where she'd been the day before. And next to her, as if he hadn't moved either, was Tom.

'It's almost like Tom's guarding her,' said Walter, caressing both cats. His voice was filled with sadness. 'Scraps has had a tiny bit to eat and some water, but that was last night. Since then she's refused everything – even cheese, which she's never turned down before.'

'She's probably still feeling very nauseous,' explained Mr Hope. 'So the last thing she'll want is food. Just keep offering her water.'

'Aye, I've been doing that,' said Walter. He paused as a worried frown spread across his face. 'This kidney trouble she's got . . . it's not, er . . . catching is it?'

Mr Hope shook his head. 'Not at all.'

Walter let out a small sigh of relief. 'It's just that Tom seems to have gone off his food too,' he said.

'I'm sure it's nothing to worry about,' said Adam Hope, looking closely at the tomcat. 'He seems to be in good shape.'

'Is Missie all right?' Mandy asked, glancing around for Walter's other cat.

'She's fine. Fussy as ever but still eating if I give

her what she likes,' said Walter, with a faint smile.

Mandy knelt down and gently scratched Tom under his chin. 'You're probably just being sympathetic and don't want to eat in front of Scraps,' she said.

Mr Hope gave Scraps another injection to help with the nausea, then he and Mandy left Walter stroking the ginger cat over and over, as if he could will his old friend to get better.

In a melancholy mood, they paddled past the marooned pub. The sadness of seeing the old cat nearing the end of her days made everything seem so much more dismal. Mandy could feel the heaviness of the depressing hush that hung over the normally lively village. There was no laughter bubbling out from the pub windows; no cheerful greetings ringing out across the street. Just the sound of the oars swishing as they cut through the water.

Mandy glanced back. Christmas would be very bleak for Walter. *It's going to be bad enough for the rest of us with all the flooding and no electricity*, she thought. *But with Scraps so ill, it's going to be even worse for Walter*.

Lost in thought, Mandy stopped concentrating

on her oar until her father's voice brought her back to reality. 'Watch out, Mandy,' he said loudly. 'You're catching crabs!'

Mandy looked down at her paddle and saw that it was missing the water altogether. 'Sorry, Dad,' she said, correcting her stroke.

'We're going to be paddling upstream to the farm now,' said Mr Hope. 'It'll be hard work with the current flowing against us so you'll need to keep your wits about you.'

Together, they pulled rhythmically on the oars and were soon gliding smoothly through the rushing water.

'At this rate, we'll be champion rowers in no time,' puffed Mr Hope. 'We'll be able to take on anyone in a boat race.'

'Oh yes,' Mandy grinned. 'Like the Oxford and Cambridge teams!'

'Absolutely!' chuckled Mr Hope. 'They wouldn't stand a chance against us.'

A pair of ducks went past them, floating effortlessly on the current. 'They don't look at all put out by the floods,' Mandy observed.

'On the contrary,' grinned Mr Hope. 'They're having a great time.'

The ducks drifted away and were almost out of sight when Mandy heard a high-pitched bark, followed by a yell. Then she saw a dinghy appearing from behind a half-submerged hedge about thirty metres downstream. 'It's James,' she said. 'And Blackie!'

James was sculling hard towards them, with Blackie leaning over the prow, barking at the ducks. The light rubber dinghy pitched and tossed as the big dog bounced up and down excitedly.

'He'll tip the boat over at that rate,' Mandy laughed. 'Or even puncture the rubber with his nails.'

'Sit, Blackie,' commanded James loudly. But Blackie ignored him, finding the ducks much more interesting.

'Need some help?' Mandy called.

'Yes, please – some calming medicine for dogs!' shouted James with a grin.

'Where are you going?' Mandy asked, trying not to upset the rhythm of her stroke.

'I was trying to catch up with you,' said James. 'Where are *you* going?'

'To Garland Farm,' Mandy explained. 'To check on an injured cow. Do you want to come too?'

'I'll try,' said James, grimacing as Blackie sat down heavily, making the dinghy rock from side to side. 'But I might end up *swimming* there!'

Mandy and her dad slowed down until James was only a few metres behind them.

'Phew! It's hard work rowing a heavy lump like Blackie upstream,' panted James.

'You should try rowing Mandy!' chuckled Mr Hope.

Mandy glared playfully at her father. 'You said just now that we made a good team,' she reminded him.

They rowed on out of the village and through a landscape they hardly recognised. There were sheets of silvery water everywhere, some of them stretching almost as far as the eye could see.

'I should think we're almost on a par with the Lake District now,' said Adam Hope, shaking his head in amazement. 'Who'd have thought our little river could burst its banks so dramatically?'

Despite the damp, chilly air, they were all rather hot from the exertion of rowing by the time they reached the farm.

'Just as well the farmhouse is on high ground,' pointed out Adam Hope.

They dragged the two boats out of the water on to a slope in a muddy field. Nearby was a big heap of broken roof timbers and splintered planks.

'That's all that's left of the old barn,' said Mr Hope.

They trudged past the collapsed building and through the soggy pastures towards the farmhouse and the temporary barn that was sheltering Mr Garland's herd of jersey cows.

Blackie seemed delighted to be able to run about on solid land again. He pulled so hard at the end of his lead that he managed to slip his collar. In a split second he was charging off into the distance, his paws kicking up clods of mud behind him.

'Come back, Blackie!' yelled James. He whistled frantically but Blackie was oblivious to James's call. He hurtled away, not once even glancing back at him.

'I guess I'd better go after him,' sighed James, heading out across the field.

'See you in about a year,' Mandy laughed, as Blackie faded to a black dot under the far hedge.

The makeshift barn was a lean-to at the side of

the farmhouse. The farmer had seen the Hopes arriving and came out to meet them.

'Thanks for going to all this trouble to reach us again,' said Mr Garland. 'I really appreciate it, and so will the heifer.'

'It's what we're here for,' smiled Mr Hope as they entered the shed. Inside, eight cows clustered together in the middle, feeding contentedly on a pile of fresh hay. At the far end of the shed, roped off from the others, was the injured heifer.

Mandy noticed at once the deep gashes on her back and shoulders. 'Ouch!' she exclaimed sympathetically. 'Those cuts look really painful.'

'You should have seen how bad they were when I first saw her,' said her dad. He examined the wounds to make sure they hadn't become infected. The heifer flinched as he touched her, but otherwise stood trustingly while Mr Hope attended to her.

Mandy massaged the cow's neck and spoke softly. 'You'll soon be feeling better,' she promised.

Relaxing under the soothing touch, the heifer fixed her big, liquid brown eyes on Mandy. Then she pushed her head forward and gave Mandy a velvety lick right across her face.

'Thanks!' Mandy spluttered, wiping her face. 'Just what I needed – a big wet kiss!'

'Looks like she's feeling a lot better already and she's saying thank you!' laughed the farmer.

Mr Hope prepared a syringe then injected the heifer's rump. 'She may *think* she's feeling better,' he said, vigorously rubbing the spot where the needle had gone in. 'But these wounds will take some time to heal. You're going to have to clean them out every day to make sure no infection sets in,' he advised, giving the farmer a tube of antiseptic ointment.

They left the cow and went outside. James was trudging back across the fields towards them with Blackie straining at the end of his leash.

'Poor James,' Mandy grinned, as he approached them. 'You look worn out.'

'I am,' said James, wiping a few specks of mud off his glasses. 'It's like I've been in some kind of marathon after all that rowing and running!'

'Well, before you start the next leg of the race why don't you all come in for a cup of tea and a mince pie?' Mr Garland asked.

'Sounds good to me,' said Mr Hope.

While they were taking their wellies off on the

porch of the small farmhouse, Mr Garland turned
to James. 'Would you mind leaving your dog out
here?' he asked him. 'You see, we're a bit full up
indoors.'

'Sure,' said James, looping Blackie's leash
around a pillar then tying a strong knot in it.

Mandy wondered what Mr Garland meant. She
didn't think he had a very big family. But as they
went into the cosy kitchen, she quickly
understood. The place was full of cats! There
were three lying on a mat in front of the cooker,
and two sprawled out on the kitchen table.
Behind the door, a plump grey cat was curled
up in a basket of clean laundry, while another
peeped out from behind a box. Mandy thought
she'd seen them all until two young tabbies came
scampering into the kitchen and began wrestling
playfully in front of her.

'You must love cats,' Mandy said, looking round
in amazement.

'Oh, I do. Although they're not really pets,' said
Mr Garland. 'They're barn cats. But when the
building collapsed the other night, I had to bring
them in here.'

'Lucky none of them was hurt,' remarked James,

bending down to smooth the cat in the laundry basket.

'Aye. These are all fine,' agreed the farmer. 'But I did lose one of them.' He filled the kettle with water. 'There's been no sign of her since that night. She might have run away in terror, I suppose, or she could even have been washed away.' He lit a match and held it against one of the rings on the gas cooker.

Washed away! The words struck a chord in Mandy. 'Was she a black and white cat?' she asked.

'Yes. A young spayed one, about six months old,' said the farmer, putting the kettle over the flame. 'The sister of those two tabbies playing over there.'

'Did you have any barrels in the barn?' Mandy continued.

'Just one,' replied Mr Garland, looking puzzled. 'Funnily enough, some of the cats liked to sleep in it.'

Mandy was elated. 'Your cat's fine,' she said, smiling broadly. 'She's just a bit scared. And at the moment, she's safe and sound in my bedroom at Animal Ark!'

Six

'Animal Ark?' echoed the farmer, his eyes wide with surprise. 'How on earth did she get there?'

'By barrel!' Mandy smiled. 'I found her floating past our front door.'

The farmer was astounded. 'I'm glad to hear she's OK,' he said, shaking his head slowly from side to side. 'But who would have believed she'd end up on the other side of the village?'

James was frowning as if trying to work something out. He pushed his glasses up his nose and said, 'Actually, it's not that hard to believe. Especially with the river flooding right up to the barn as well as all the way to Animal Ark.'

'Sounds logical,' agreed Mr Hope. 'And when you think how strong both the wind and the current must have been, it's no wonder the barrel travelled such a distance.'

James turned to Mandy. 'Just as well you came here today,' he said. 'Otherwise it might have taken us ages to find out where Flicker came from.'

Mandy was already picturing the happy reunion of the little black and white cat with the others. 'She's going to be so pleased to be back with her own family,' she agreed.

The farmer was pouring boiling water into a teapot. He stopped and turned to Mandy with an uncomfortable look on his face. 'Actually,' he began, then cleared his throat. 'I'm not sure if . . .' He hesitated again. 'You see . . . Well, the thing is, I just don't have the room to take her back,' he said, his words now tumbling out in a rush. 'And with a sick cow and all the repairs I have to do around here, I don't think I'll have the time to care for her properly, especially if she's not well either.'

'But she's not ill,' Mandy protested. 'Just a bit shaken. She'll be fine when she's back where she belongs.'

The farmer shrugged his shoulders. 'I'm very sorry. I just don't think I can fit another animal in here right now. You can see how over-run I am.' He looked at Adam Hope. 'And anyway, I'd already been thinking of trying to find homes for some of the cats. You couldn't find a new owner for her, could you?' he asked hopefully.

Adam Hope tugged at his beard. 'It's hard to say. Everyone's very busy at the moment.'

'And right now, everyone's flooded out,' pointed out James. 'No one's going to want to make things more complicated by taking in a new pet.'

'And what about Flicker's feelings?' Mandy protested, thinking of the cat's timid nature. 'Imagine what it would be like for her, to be pushed from pillar to post after all that's happened. She *deserves* to feel safe and to be with people and cats that she trusts.'

But Mr Garland was adamant. 'I really haven't got the room at the moment,' he insisted. 'And it'll be ages before I can build a new barn.' He pointed to the grey cat in the basket. 'On top of everything, that one's expecting kittens in a week or two.' He looked at Mandy again. 'And like you said, Flicker needs a loving home. I just can't give her that right now.'

Mandy felt a wave of frustration rising in her. *The floods have ruined everything*, she thought angrily. She stared out at the turbulent water rushing past the shattered timbers of the barn. *If I could keep her, I would*, she told herself. But she knew that it wasn't possible. If they took in all the strays and abandoned animals that came to Animal Ark, they'd soon be overwhelmed.

Adam Hope put an arm around Mandy's shoulder. 'Mr Garland has to be practical,' he said kindly. 'And, anyway, I don't think Flicker would welcome another journey across water just now.' He picked up his vet's bag and turned to the farmer. 'Don't worry. We'll look after her for the time being and try to find a home for her.'

'I'll ask round these parts,' said Mr Garland. 'Some of the neighbouring farmers might want a good barn cat.'

On their way down to the boats, Mandy tried to convince herself that it really was in Flicker's best interests to go to a new home. *But it will have to be a very special one*, she told herself. *She's used to a quiet life in the barn and lots of cats as companions*. Mandy thought how shy Flicker was. Most people wanted confident, affectionate cats. Who would be prepared to take on such a timid little creature?

Mandy turned to James. 'Dad's right when he says it's not going to be easy to find a home for Flicker.'

'That means we'd better start looking for one as soon as we can,' said James, dragging his dinghy towards the water.

'Did you tell Mrs McFarlane about Flicker earlier, James?' Mandy asked, as she and her father hauled their boat along too.

'No. I haven't been to the post office yet,' James answered. 'I'll go there now on my way home.' He stopped at the edge of the water and urged Blackie to jump into the dinghy. 'Sit, boy,' he commanded after the dog leaped easily into the boat. 'And keep still this time. You nearly had me in the water when you saw those ducks.'

The Labrador sat, then wagged his tail expectantly.

'And keep those paws still,' added James. 'Those sharp nails of yours could easily puncture the boat.'

'I'm surprised they didn't do that earlier – the way he was clambering all over it,' Mandy remarked. She sized up the dinghy. There was just enough room for another person. 'I think I should come with you to Mrs McFarlane's, seeing as I know what Flicker looks like,' she suggested to James. 'I can write a description of her to put up in the post office.'

'OK,' agreed James. 'Then we'll go back to Animal Ark and you can introduce me to Flicker before I paddle home again.'

Mandy started to climb into the dinghy.

'Hey! This is mutiny,' announced Adam Hope, standing next to the rowing boat with his hands on his hips. 'Abandoning me and my boat like this.'

'It's for a good cause, Dad,' Mandy laughed.

'Good cause, nothing!' he retorted. 'You're supposed to be my galley-slave.'

'Since when?' joked Mandy in return. 'You're forgetting that you called me a heavy lump earlier.'

'Well, we're not going upstream now. We'll be paddling with the current,' said Mr Hope, winking at James. 'And for that, I need some ballast to keep me stable.'

'Then take Blackie,' chuckled James.

'Blackie! Not on your life. He'll keep the boat about as stable as a leaf in a whirlpool,' said Mr Hope, climbing into the boat and picking up the oars. 'I shall just have to go it alone.'

They paddled back along the swollen river. In her mind, Mandy pictured Flicker's barrel being swept along the same route. It was just sheer luck that the raging waters hadn't carried the cat right past Animal Ark, to who knew where.

For a while, the two boats kept abreast of one another, but eventually they drifted apart as the current bore the rowing boat ahead of the heavily laden dinghy.

Mandy and James steered the little rubber boat along, watching out for the flood debris that was being washed downstream. In contrast to the journey out to the farm, Blackie was very well-behaved. He sat motionless in the stern, watching the passing landscape.

'It's just as well that he went running off like that and used up some of his energy,' Mandy said. 'I think he's too tired to move.'

'I wonder about that,' said James, narrowing his eyes as he looked at Blackie. 'If I know him, he's plotting something really big. Like how to make the boat capsize.'

'You wouldn't do a thing like that, would you, Blackie?' Mandy grinned.

Hearing his name, the Labrador suddenly stood up and took a step towards Mandy. The dinghy started rocking wildly.

'See what I mean,' gasped James, pulling up his oar and holding it in front of the dog to stop him moving forward again. 'Sit, Blackie!' he said sternly. '*SIT*!'

Blackie looked at him in surprise, as if he couldn't believe James could be so firm.

'SIT!' James commanded again.

But Blackie remained standing. Then without any warning, he shook himself vigorously, spraying jets of muddy water off his coat and all over Mandy and James.

The dinghy pitched and tossed so violently that water seeped in over the sides.

Mandy dug in her oar, trying to steady the boat. 'Blackie, sit!' she said. At last, the big black dog sat down in the puddle of water that was now swishing about in the bottom of the boat.

James took a deep breath. 'You'll be the end

of me.' He stopped. 'I think we'd better avoid his name until we're on dry land,' he said to Mandy.

Before long, the surging river brought them to the flooded village green.

'I think the water's dropped a bit,' observed Mandy. 'This morning, it was almost up to the top step of the pub. And now you can actually see the next step down.'

'That's right,' agreed James. 'But where's the Christmas tree?' he demanded suddenly, blinking once as if he couldn't believe his eyes.

Mandy stared at where the tree had been anchored just a few hours before. There was no sign of it now. 'It must have been washed away,' she said with disappointment. 'The carol service tomorrow evening isn't going to be the same without a tree to sing around.'

'If there *is* a carol service with all this water about,' James pointed out. 'Even if the water has started going down, there's no way it'll have gone completely by tomorrow night.' He stood his oar upright in the water until the blade touched the ground. The water reached halfway up the paddle. 'See? It must be about half a metre deep still. No one's going to want to stand up to their waists in cold water to sing carols!'

'No carol service, no decorations, no tree, no lights. That means no Christmas, I guess,' Mandy murmured dejectedly.

Then, as if to highlight just how miserable things were, Julian Hardy, the landlord of the Fox and Goose, and his eleven-year-old son, John, came out of the front door and started gathering up the fairy lights. The lights had slipped down from the eaves and were dangling so close to the ground that they were in danger of falling into the water.

Julian saw Mandy and James paddling across the submerged green. He waved to them and called, 'Nice to see some people out and about!' He began winding the string of lights around one arm. 'Pity you weren't here a little earlier. I could have used a dinghy.'

'Why?' asked James, steering the boat closer to the pub.

'To rescue the Christmas tree,' explained John. 'We saw the rope breaking and tried to wade out to grab it, but we were too late. We might have managed if we'd had a boat.'

'I suppose the tree's well on its way to the North

Sea by now,' Mandy said glumly, lifting her oar clear of the water as the dinghy became wedged against a hedge.

'I don't think so,' said James. He was leaning over the side of the boat, scrutinising the water. Blackie leaned across too, as if he were trying to make out what James was looking at.

'Well, at least heading out of Welford then,' Mandy persisted, holding on to Blackie's collar in case he decided to jump into the water. 'And anyway it doesn't really matter, because it's gone.'

James looked round at her. 'It hasn't,' he said. 'It's right here, caught in the hedge. You can just see one branch sticking out of the water.'

Mandy looked to where James was pointing. 'You're right,' she said, seeing the tip of a branch just visible above the water.

Julian craned his neck until he spotted the tree too. 'Well, even if it isn't on its way to Denmark, it's still no good to us like that.'

'It's better than nothing,' said James, trying to sound cheerful.

'We could try and rescue it now,' suggested John.

Julian looked doubtfully at the submerged tree. 'I don't know how, with the current still so strong,' he said.

Mandy and James left the Hardys trying to work out how to salvage the tree and paddled on to the post office. Mandy went in, leaving James in the dinghy with Blackie because dogs weren't allowed inside.

The bell rang cheerfully as Mandy pushed open the door. 'Be with you in a sec!' called Mrs McFarlane from the back.

Mandy heard a door closing then Mrs McFarlane appeared, drying her hands on a towel.

'I've just been sweeping some water off the back porch,' she said. 'Thank goodness the rain's stopped at last. Let's hope that's the end of it now.'

Mandy gave her James's list of groceries then told her about Flicker. 'Could I put a notice up in here asking about a new home for her?' she asked.

'Of course,' said Mrs McFarlane. She gave Mandy a sheet of paper and a felt-tipped pen. 'But there won't exactly be crowds reading it right now. You and James are practically the only customers I've had since the flooding started!'

'But when the flooding is over, there'll be floods of people coming in because they'll have run out of things at home by then,' Mandy smiled. 'And then they'll read about Flicker. Someone's bound to want her.'

'Let's hope so,' said Mrs McFarlane.

While Mandy made the notice, Mrs McFarlane fetched all the items on the list and packed them into several plastic carrier bags. 'Can you manage?' she asked, giving them to Mandy.

'We'll be fine,' Mandy told her, going towards the door. 'As long as Blackie behaves himself.'

After the strenuous row to the farm earlier that day, the short journey from the village to Animal

Ark seemed very easy. Before long, and with their arms aching from the exertion of rowing for most of the morning, the two friends came to the end of the driveway. Mandy looked up as they paddled under the sign and saw a shaft of sunshine and a patch of blue sky in the west. It cheered her up enormously. 'Enough blue sky to make a sailor a new suit,' she smiled, remembering one of her gran's sayings. 'That means it's definitely clearing up.'

'Great!' said James. 'That'll make it easier for us to find a home for Flicker.' He jiggled his oar in the water to get rid of a plastic bag that had become wrapped around the blade. 'I can't wait to meet her.'

'She's really sweet,' Mandy told him. 'But don't forget she's also very shy, so she might not let you go anywhere near her just yet.'

They paddled into the garden and as they neared the house, James stared at the brightly coloured flotilla of rowing boats bobbing about. 'It reminds me of a marina,' he joked. 'I feel like I'm on holiday. Now all we need is some bright sunshine and lots of people . . .' He paused as something dawned on him. 'I've got it!' he burst out. 'We *can* have the carol service after all. We can use the rowing boats to get everyone there!'

'That's a brilliant idea!' Mandy declared, punching the air so enthusiastically that the dinghy reeled and tossed. 'Oops!' she said, holding the sides of the boat as it gradually stopped rocking.

Blackie put his head to one side and looked at her quizzically. 'OK, boy,' Mandy laughed. 'You're not the only one to rock the boat. I'm in the dog house too!' Then, beaming happily at James, she went on, 'I can just imagine what it will be like. We've got enough boats for the whole of Welford to float on the green. Even without the Christmas tree, it'll be the best carol service ever!'

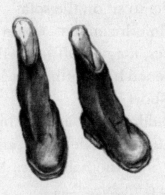

Seven

'We'll have to ask the boat company for permission, of course,' Mandy realised, as they wedged the dinghy against the rowing boat on the front porch.

'Yes. And right now we'd better ask your mum and dad for permission to take Blackie indoors,' added James, holding the dog's collar to stop him plunging off the steps and back into the water. Even though the Labrador had already shaken off a lot of mud and water, his coat was still very damp.

'They won't mind,' Mandy said. 'As long as he

doesn't expect to sit on the sofa!'

'You wouldn't dream of it, would you, Blackie?' grinned James, tugging off his wellies.

Blackie opened his mouth in a wide doggy grin then gave a short bark.

'Butter wouldn't melt in your mouth,' Mandy chuckled, patting Blackie's head affectionately.

They went into the hall where Mandy dialled the boat hire company.

'It's a grand idea,' said Andrew Bond enthusiastically when Mandy explained what they had in mind. 'And I tell you what, I'll come round in one of my other boats to give you a hand. I love a good singsong.'

'Thank you. That's really kind,' Mandy said. She hung up and told James about Mr Bond's offer.

'That will make things easier,' said James as they went through to the kitchen. 'I was wondering how we'd move all the boats by ourselves. Now the next thing is to tell everyone about it.'

'What are you two plotting now?' asked Emily Hope, who was sitting on a chair with Stardust in her lap. She looked at Blackie and frowned, then quickly returned the chinchilla to the safety of her cage. 'Better not take any risks,' she said.

'We're organising a really great carol service,' Mandy said, reaching her fingers through the bars and rubbing Stardust's chest.

Mr Hope was busy making a pile of sandwiches. He looked up from the table and said suspiciously, 'Not on board Animal Ark, I hope.'

'No. On board the rowing boats,' responded James.

'You mean, everyone's going to be floating about our garden singing Christmas carols?' asked Adam Hope, looking confused.

Mandy shook her head. 'No, Dad. They're all going to the village green,' she laughed. 'We'll tow the boats to people and they can row there.'

'It's a terrific idea,' said Mrs Hope. 'But let's hope other people think so too. After all, it's still rather grim outdoors.'

'It's going to be much better tomorrow,' Mandy said positively. Turning to James, she said, 'Come and meet Flicker.'

They left Blackie with Mr and Mrs Hope and went upstairs. Mandy opened her bedroom door cautiously and peeped inside. Flicker was asleep on her bed but sensed Mandy coming in. The timid cat's eyes shot open and she watched warily as Mandy came over to her.

'I see what you mean,' whispered James. 'She really is shy.' He stopped at the door. 'I'll wait here to give her a chance to get used to me.'

'It's all right, Flicker,' Mandy crooned. She sat on the edge of her bed and held a hand out to the cat. Flicker sniffed it hesitantly.

'You're going to have to get a lot braver,' Mandy said, slowly moving her hand forward to smooth the cat. 'Otherwise it'll be really difficult to find you a home.'

Flicker shrank back.

'She's not a very good advertisement for herself,' agreed James quietly from the door.

'No,' Mandy said. 'But I bet she'd be OK if she was with her friends.' She tried once more to touch Flicker. To her surprise, the cat kept still this time and allowed Mandy to stroke her lightly.

'There. That's not so bad, is it?' Mandy said. But she could feel Flicker's muscles tensing as she smoothed her. 'A purr would be an even better reaction,' she said to James. 'Let's see if she'll let you come closer now.'

She kept smoothing Flicker as James

approached. But before James was halfway across the room, the cat suddenly leaped to the floor and dived under the bed.

James shrugged good-naturedly. 'I guess you just need your space at the moment,' he said, then added, 'And we could do with some of those sandwiches your dad was making, Mandy. I'm starving after all that rowing.'

'You're *always* starving,' Mandy teased as they closed the door on Flicker then went downstairs.

Over lunch, the two friends discussed how they'd tell the Welford community about the floating carol service.

'I could ring Gran,' Mandy suggested, going across to Stardust whose cage was safely out of Blackie's reach on the dresser. 'She can tell the Women's Institute about it, and they can tell all their friends.' Mandy's gran, Dorothy Hope, was the chairwoman of the local W.I. and could always be relied on to spread important news.

'And we can row back to the post office after lunch,' said James, 'to put up another notice.'

'I was just going to suggest that myself,' Mandy grinned. 'And I'll take the rowing boat so you don't have to come all the way back here afterwards.' She gave Stardust a carrot, then went back to her place at the table. 'We'll tell Julian Hardy too,' she added, pulling out her chair. 'He might be able to let a few people know.'

'Hold your horses, you two,' said Mr Hope, shaking his head. 'It's all very well to advertise your carols-in-a-rowing-boat service, but *we'll* need to find out exactly who's coming so that we know who needs a boat.'

'Good point, Dad,' Mandy said. 'I guess everyone will have to ring us up to let us know for sure.'

A look of dismay crossed Mrs Hope's face. 'Get them to ring *here*?' she echoed. 'Not on your life. We need to keep the lines clear in case of emergencies.' As if to underline her point, the phone started ringing.

While Mrs Hope was answering the phone, Mr Hope came up with a suggestion to solve their problem. 'We can ask Gran to be the co-ordinator,' he said. 'You know how efficient she is. People can let her know and she can make a list for us.'

'I'm sure she'll love that,' Mandy said. 'Gran's a great organiser.'

As soon as Mrs Hope came back into the

kitchen, Mandy and James went to ring Gran to put her in the picture.

'Now that sounds like an exciting event,' said Gran at the other end of the line. 'Just what Welford needs after all this miserable weather! I'll get on to it right away,' she promised. 'The Christmas group will be a good bunch to start the ball rolling.' In addition to belonging to the W.I., Gran was also on the committee that organised the Christmas party in the village hall. 'Mrs Ponsonby and the other members are probably expecting to get off lightly this year,' she chuckled merrily. 'I'll have them working the phones in no time at all.'

'Thanks, Gran,' Mandy said. 'We knew we could count on you.'

Back in the kitchen, Mandy and James helped to wash up while Blackie polished off the scraps left over from lunch.

'Nice to have an automatic vacuum cleaner,' smiled Mr Hope, giving Blackie a half-eaten egg sandwich.

'He takes after his owner,' Mandy teased, ducking as James flicked his tea towel at her. Then, looking at her watch, she said, 'We'd better get moving if we're going back to the village. Otherwise I'll end up rowing home in the dark.'

Mrs Hope looked across at Stardust who was nibbling contentedly on the carrot. 'I wonder . . .' she began.

'Yes, love?' prompted Adam Hope.

'Well, that was Stardust's owner on the phone earlier,' said Mrs Hope. 'The family's missing her a lot and would love to have her home for Christmas. But their house is right near the river so even if the water drops a bit, it might be days before they can get here.'

'And you're wondering if I'll take Stardust home in a rowing boat?' Mandy said, reading her mother's thoughts.

Mrs Hope nodded. 'If you put her cage on the seat next to you, she should stay dry,' she said.

'I've got a better idea,' Mandy said, remembering how the barrel had kept Flicker safe the night before. 'We can put her cage inside the plastic laundry basket. Then she won't even *see* the water around us, let alone get wet.'

Mrs Hope rang up Stardust's owners to tell them the good news, then Mandy and James put

Blackie and Stardust into the two boats and set off for the village.

'It's a proper floating circus,' laughed Adam Hope as the two friends paddled away – James and Blackie in the dinghy and Mandy and Stardust in the rowing boat.

The first stop was Stardust's home. Mandy handed Stardust over to Beth, who was over the moon to have her pet back again.

'Make sure you keep her really warm and dry while all this water's still about,' Mandy advised, before she and James paddled on again.

In the prow of the dinghy, Blackie stood very still, staring straight ahead with an alert expression on his face.

'He looks like a ship's figurehead,' Mandy called across to James.

'Well, I don't trust him to keep still,' said James. 'I bet he's on the lookout for more ducks.' To their relief, no ducks swam across their path and Blackie was still standing calmly when they rowed into the village centre.

As before, Welford was almost deserted. The only people about were Julian and his wife Sara, who was John's step-mother. They were sweeping water away from the front door of the Fox and Goose. When Julian saw them paddling over, he rested his hands on the top of the broom. 'Ahoy there!' he called cheerfully to them. 'Back again so soon! Nothing keeps you two still for long, does it? Not even these floods!'

'Actually, that's why we're back,' Mandy told him. 'We're going to turn the floods into the best Christmas ever!' She outlined their plans for the carol service.

'Now that's what I call a real celebration!' enthused Sara, shaking water from her broom.

'It should be great fun,' agreed Julian. 'I'll tell everyone I speak to.' He glanced over to where the Christmas tree was protruding out of the water and then up to the bare eaves above him. 'Pity about the tree and the fairy lights. But I guess we'll just have to make do without them this year.'

Mandy and James were about to continue to the post office, when they saw the wiry figure of Ernie Bell wading through the water down the lane next to the pub. He was wearing green rubber boots which went all the way to the tops of his legs.

'Those are brilliant wellies,' James called to the

retired carpenter. 'Almost as good as a dinghy for getting around.'

'I found these in a jumble sale back in the summer,' said Mr Bell, his face creased into its usual frown. 'I knew they'd come in handy one day.' He made his way to the front of the pub and sloshed up the stairs to stand next to Julian and Sara.

'How are Sammy and Tiddles?' Mandy asked,

letting her boat drift into the car park where it came to a standstill against a big rhododendron bush.

Sammy was Ernie's pet squirrel which he kept in a run in his back garden, and Tiddles was his kitten.

'They're both fine,' said Ernie. 'Mind you, I had to make a temporary run in my kitchen for Sammy. It's a bit cramped indoors now but I'm luckier than some,' he said, glancing meaningfully back down the lane towards the little cottages where both he and Walter Pickard lived. 'At least all my animals are in good shape.'

Mandy nodded understandingly. 'I suppose we could hope for a miracle for Scraps,' she said, even though she knew the chances of one were very remote.

'Aye. That's what I said to Walter when I popped in on my way here,' said Ernie gravely. 'But he's no fool. He knew I was only trying to cheer him up.'

Mandy sighed and looked down the lane. Tears pricked the corners of her eyes as she thought about poor Scraps. She brushed them away with the back of one hand. 'I don't think anything can cheer him up now,' she said, turning her gaze away from the cottages. 'Not even the carol service.'

'But that's cancelled anyway,' said Ernie.

'Not any more,' said James, who had also drifted into the car park and was holding on to a window sill.

They filled Ernie in about the service. He listened silently then agreed to join in. 'But I won't be here if it starts raining again,' he said grumpily. 'I'm not one for standing about singing in the rain, you know.'

'You won't be standing about,' Mandy corrected him with a smile. 'You'll be floating about.'

'We'll see about that,' muttered Ernie.

Mandy and James's next stop was the post office. As before, James waited outside with Blackie while Mandy went in to tell Mrs McFarlane about their plan, and to put a poster up alongside the one advertising Flicker.

'Now you're sure you won't be back to put up any more notices today?' laughed Mrs McFarlane when Mandy turned to go.

'I hope not,' said Mandy above the jangle of the bell as she opened the door. 'I need a bit of a rest from rowing.'

Satisfied that they'd done as much as they could

to spread the word about the carol service, Mandy and James turned for home.

'I'll phone after lunch tomorrow,' said James. 'By then, your gran should have the list ready for us.'

The two friends then went their separate ways. Darkness was already falling by the time Mandy arrived at Animal Ark. She felt a pang as she approached the dark stone cottage. No warm lights filtered out from the windows to welcome her home. And inside, the only sign that it was nearly Christmas was a drooping artificial tree and a few strings of tinsel.

In the living room, Adam Hope was lighting a fire. 'Mum's upstairs checking on Flicker,' he told Mandy. 'I tried to see to the cat myself, but she wouldn't let me near her.'

'Sounds familiar,' Mandy said. 'She gave James the same treatment.'

She went up to her room. Mrs Hope was crouching on the floor, trying to entice Flicker out from under the bed with a bowl of chicken pieces. There was a new candle in the jar that had served as a nightlight for Flicker the night before. But unlike then, the timid cat no longer seemed to find the light comforting.

'She's not giving an inch,' said Emily Hope, sitting on the floor.

Mandy knelt down next to her. 'She let me stroke her this morning,' she said. 'But she wasn't very happy about it.'

'Perhaps we're putting too much pressure on her,' said Mrs Hope. She stood up and took the dish of chicken over to the other food bowl in the corner. Flicker had barely touched the food that had been there since the morning. 'She might prefer to be entirely alone for a while.'

'You mean put her in the residential unit?' Mandy asked.

'Yes,' said Mrs Hope.

'But she'll be really lonely in there,' Mandy protested. 'At least until we start having patients coming in again.'

'I know,' said Mrs Hope. 'And that's why now's the time to put her in there. Sometimes a traumatised animal just needs a bit of time and space to recover. If we keep pressing her, expecting her to be friendly and happy, she may start feeling hunted.'

Mandy saw the sense in her mother's

argument. If she tried to force the little cat to make friends, Flicker might retreat even further into herself. And then no one would ever give her a home. 'Let's leave her in here for one more night,' she said, still hoping that Flicker might become used to having her around. 'If she's not more confident by the morning, I'll put her in the residential unit.'

Later, while putting fresh sand into the litter tray, Mandy couldn't help wishing that Mr Garland would take Flicker back. It certainly looked like the only solution.

She carried the tray upstairs then stretched out on her stomach and looked at Flicker. The cat stared back out at her from under the bed, her green eyes flashing in the dancing candlelight.

'You're really no trouble at all,' Mandy said softly to her. 'Just a bit shy.'

Flicker twitched her ears and blinked.

'And Mr Garland said you're a really good mouser,' Mandy went on. She stood up and went over to the door then paused and looked back over her shoulder. Flicker was still watching her intently. 'Perhaps when all the flooding is over and things are back to normal, Mr Garland will agree to take you back,' Mandy said. And she resolved right then to do her best to persuade him to let Flicker go home.

Eight

Mandy's heart sank when she drew back the curtains the next morning. It was raining again!

'Oh no!' she groaned. 'This will spoil everything if it goes on all day.' She searched the sky for a break in the low grey clouds, but there wasn't even a hint of blue. *So much for the sailor's new suit*, Mandy thought irritably.

Flicker was also awake. She had spent the night at the foot of the bed but jumped down as soon as Mandy stirred. Now she was hunched over the food bowl in the corner, picking half-heartedly at the contents.

'Come on, Flicker,' Mandy encouraged her in a low voice. 'You can do better than that. You've hardly eaten a thing since you washed up here in your barrel. I bet you're ravenous really.'

But any hunger Flicker had took second place to her anxiety. While she ate, she looked around tensely, her ears pricked for the slightest noise. She was taking no chances. She was clearly poised to flee at any moment.

'Will you *ever* get over your big fright?' Mandy wondered aloud, pulling on some jeans and a thick sweater. She longed to see the cat contented and at ease. And if only she'd let Mandy cuddle her, like she'd done when she was in shock that first night. That would be a big breakthrough. 'Maybe you'll let me pick you up this morning,' Mandy said, slowly going over to her.

But Flicker made it clear that she wanted to be left alone. She allowed Mandy to touch her briefly then she scurried off across the floor to her safe place under the bed.

'You're in real fright-and-flight mode,' Mandy mused. 'It's going to take something very special to get you out of it. In the meantime, we'll let you have your own space.'

After breakfast, Mandy went into the residential unit to prepare a cage for Flicker. She put some clean bedding in one corner then looked around for a cardboard box. *Just in case she feels vulnerable here*, she thought.

She found a suitable box, then lay it on its side in the cage. Next, she chose a fleecy blanket and put it in the box to make a cosy hiding place for Flicker. *It might just remind her of her barrel*, thought Mandy. *Before she was washed away in it.*

When the cage was ready, Mandy went to fetch Flicker. She took a wire cat basket to make sure Flicker didn't escape on her way to her new quarters.

'Sorry to have to do this to you,' Mandy said, reaching under her bed and gently dragging Flicker out. 'But it might be just what you need.'

Flicker wriggled briefly as Mandy lowered her into the basket. But once she was inside, she sat very still and stared out timidly. Mandy carried Flicker downstairs, wishing she could explain things to her. 'You probably think something really horrible is going to happen to you again,' she said.

In the residential unit, Mandy reluctantly transferred Flicker into the cage. 'I'll miss having you in my bedroom,' she said. 'And if you knew what was good for you, you'd miss me too!'

Flicker inspected her new surroundings. She was particularly interested in the cardboard box. She sniffed it inquisitively then, deciding it was safe, crept inside and curled up on the downy blanket.

'All settled?' asked Mandy's father, coming into the residential unit.

Mandy nodded. 'I think so. Now we'll just have to wait and see how she does.'

'In the meantime, there's another cat I need to see,' Mr Hope reminded her.

'Mmm. Scraps,' Mandy said. She peered in at Flicker once more. 'At least there's hope for you,' she said sombrely. 'But the future's not very bright for poor old Scraps.'

'Or for Walter right now,' added Mr Hope as he and Mandy went out of the unit. 'I think deep down he knows it's just a question of deciding on the right moment to put Scraps to sleep.'

'I hope it's not Christmas Day,' Mandy said quietly.

'I'm afraid it'll be sooner than that,' said Mr Hope.

Mandy and her dad went into a treatment room, where Mr Hope replenished his vet's bag. 'I need to ring Mr Garland first to see how the heifer is,' he said, putting some new syringes into the bag. 'Then, assuming I'm not needed at the farm, I'm going to see Scraps. Want to come with me?'

'OK,' said Mandy. 'But do me a favour please, Dad?'

'I will if I can,' answered Mr Hope.

Mandy leaned across the table in the centre of the room. 'See if you can make Mr Garland change his mind about Flicker,' she begged.

Mr Hope shook his head sympathetically. 'I wish I could, love,' he said. 'But you heard what he said. He just doesn't have the space. Not even for one more—'

'One more will make no difference,' Mandy interrupted. 'Especially one that's so quiet and timid.'

'That may be,' said Mr Hope with understanding. He snapped the bag shut and heaved it off the table. 'But you're forgetting one thing.'

'What's that?' Mandy asked, following him into the reception area.

'That a home isn't a good one if an animal isn't

really wanted there,' he said. 'And Flicker is in need of some very special care right now.'

Mandy fell silent. Her dad had a point. Still, things were different with Flicker. For Flicker, home meant being with other cats. *And that's probably another reason she's so timid*, Mandy reasoned to herself. *It's not just her bad experience. She's missing all her friends in the barn. She's not really used to being an only cat.*

Mr Hope picked up the phone.

'Just ask Mr Garland anyway,' Mandy insisted. 'He might want her back after all.'

'I really doubt it,' sighed Mr Hope as he dialled the number and waited for the farmer to answer.

But Mr Garland hadn't changed his mind. After telling Mr Hope that the cow was much better, he asked after Flicker. He was keen to know if anyone was interested in giving her a home yet, but he didn't offer to take her back.

Disappointed, Mandy followed her dad back through the cottage to the front porch. It was still raining but only lightly now. 'Do you think it'll stop by tonight?' she asked as they pulled on their rain gear.

Mr Hope shrugged. 'Who knows? There are still

a lot of clouds about, so it could get worse,' he said, climbing into the rowing boat and picking up an oar.

'Not *worse*,' Mandy protested, settling herself into the boat then slicing her oar into the water. 'Don't even *think* that.'

Paddling away from Animal Ark, she wondered how many more boat trips they'd be making before things were back to normal. She was quite used to getting about on the water now, but there were signs everywhere that the flood waters were receding. On the way to the village, Mandy and her dad saw hedges, low walls and even green stripes of meadow that hadn't been visible in days.

'It'll be great to be able to use motor power instead of muscle power again,' puffed Mr Hope as they rowed past the Fox and Goose towards Walter's cottage.

Arriving, they knocked on the door and Walter called to them to come in. 'The door's not locked,' came his gruff voice.

The atmosphere inside the little house was heavy with sadness. Walter was sitting in a chair in front of the fire with Scraps lying limply in his

lap. Tom sat on the arm of the chair, as if he was guarding his ill companion.

Walter looked up at Mandy and her dad. 'It's good of you to come,' he said, huskily. He rubbed his eyes with one hand. Mandy thought he looked very tired, as if he'd been awake for most of the night.

'Scraps is no better,' continued Walter. 'Is there something else you can give her?'

Mr Hope shook his head sadly. 'We've done all we can,' he said. 'Once the kidneys start failing, there really is no hope.' He bent down and stroked the old cat who looked at him with tired, heavy eyes.

'But she can't go yet!' blurted out Walter. 'She ate a few morsels again during the night. Maybe she's on the mend after all . . .' His voice faded away, and Mandy could tell that he knew in his heart that Scraps wasn't going to get better.

A lump formed in Mandy's throat and she had to turn away. Poor Walter. It was going to be so hard for him to have to make the final decision. *And poor Tom*, she thought. *He looks even more miserable today. He's lost weight, too.*

Mr Hope stood up and put one hand on Walter's shoulder. 'You let us know when you're ready,' he said kindly. 'But don't wait too long. We don't want Scraps to suffer any more than she has to.'

'Aye, I know,' mumbled Walter. 'I just want more time to say goodbye.' He drew the old cat closer as if trying to protect her. 'Sorry to make you go back and forth, Adam,' he said. 'But I just can't bring myself . . .'

'I know,' interrupted Mr Hope sympathetically. 'Don't hesitate to call us at any time. We'll get here as soon as we can.'

'Would you mind having another look at Tom before you go?' asked Walter, stroking the cat with one hand. 'He's worrying me a lot.'

'Still off his food?' asked Mr Hope, picking Tom up.

'Aye. He's had nothing for two days now,' said Walter.

Mr Hope put Tom on the small dining table and examined him thoroughly. 'I can't find anything wrong,' he said finally. 'But cats can be very sensitive creatures. I expect he's feeling too upset about Scraps to want to eat.'

A shadow of anguish passed across Walter's face. 'That means he'll be even worse when Scraps does . . .' He broke off.

Mandy lifted Tom off the table and hugged him to her. 'We're all very sad about Scraps,' she whispered to him. 'But it's very hard for Mr Pickard to have to worry about you too. You must try to eat, for his sake.'

Tom wriggled about until he freed himself from Mandy and jumped to the ground. Then, with an angry flick of his tail, he leaped back on to the arm of Walter's chair and resumed his vigil over Scraps.

Leaving the pitiful scene, Mandy felt very sad. She tried to think ahead to the carol service that night, but the picture of Walter and his two forlorn cats kept forcing itself into her mind.

Back at Animal Ark, Mandy went straight to the residential unit to see if Flicker was any more settled. She knelt down outside the cage and peered into the cardboard box. A pair of bright eyes peered back at her.

Mandy waited, hoping Flicker would venture out to be petted. But Flicker stayed where she was, her wary gaze set firmly on Mandy.

Mandy sat back on her heels. She shook her head and sighed. Flicker, Scraps and Tom – three cats all tearing at her heart strings at once. And right now, it seemed there was no way of helping any of them.

Nine

Mandy was delighted when Grandma Hope told her that lots of people wanted to attend the carol service. 'Just about everyone thinks it's a grand idea,' said Gran when she phoned up after lunch. 'Especially Reverend Hadcroft. He said he'd let the church choir know.'

'Dad's one member who already knows about it,' Mandy chuckled.

Gran read out her list while Mandy jotted down the names. 'Phew!' Mandy said, counting them all quickly. 'I just hope we have enough boats for everyone.'

James arrived in his dinghy after lunch. He'd brought several coiled-up ropes with him. 'I thought these might come in handy for pulling all the boats along,' he said.

'They certainly will,' said Adam Hope. 'All of our ropes are in the garage, and getting them out would mean opening the door and letting the water in.'

'Let's get started,' said Mrs Hope, pulling on her gloves and a woolly hat.

Mandy grabbed her jacket and opened the front door. The light drizzle had finally stopped, and only thick cloud cover remained.

Mandy was about to climb into the dinghy, but she paused as she heard an unfamiliar droning sound coming from somewhere down the lane. 'What's that?' she wondered.

The noise was coming closer.

'It sounds like a motor,' James said, squinting into the distance to see if he could spot what it was.

Emily Hope frowned. 'Surely it's not a car coming up the lane?'

'Not unless it's an amphibious one,' said Mr Hope with a smile.

The mystery was cleared up a moment later. Mandy was the first to see what it was. 'Look!' she exclaimed, pointing down the driveway.

A long motorised punt was gliding into the garden. And steering it through the water to the cottage was Andrew Bond. 'Good afternoon, all,' he called out cheerfully, as he pulled up in front of them and quelled the engine.

'That's a terrific boat,' said James, looking enviously at the powerful engine.

'Yes. I thought it would be more useful than another rowing boat,' said Mr Bond. 'As you can see, there's room for quite a few people in here.'

'It'll be ideal for the choir,' suggested Adam Hope.

'We were just about to rope the boats together,' Emily Hope told Mr Bond. 'And I think we could do with a practised hand.'

'No problem,' replied the boat owner. 'We'll have them strung out behind us in a jiffy.' He picked up a boat hook from the floor of the punt. 'I'll pull them over, Adam, and you can attach them all to each other.'

Before long, there were four strings of brightly coloured rowing boats bobbing about on the water

– one each for Mandy, James and Adam and Emily Hope to tow into the village. Andrew Bond double-checked that all the boats were securely fastened, then he went ahead in the punt to collect the choir. Emily Hope had drawn a map for him to show where everyone lived, and put it in a transparent plastic bag to keep dry.

'Let's set sail, everyone,' chuckled Adam Hope. He pushed his oars into the water and struck out towards the lane. With a jerk, his line of little boats lurched off behind him, bumping and knocking against each other in the choppy water.

Mandy set off next. She'd gone only a few metres when she heard the sound of a helicopter flying overhead. She glanced up. The helicopter was low enough for her to see the pilot. He was looking down out of his side window at the scene below him.

'He must wonder what on earth we're up to,' she called over her shoulder to James who was just behind her.

'Yes. It must look really weird,' laughed James.

The helicopter circled once to get another look at the convoy of little boats. Mandy waved at the pilot, who returned her greeting then continued on his way north.

The Hopes and James paddled on, separating eventually to drop off the boats. By the time they had delivered them all, it was starting to get dark. Mandy fetched her friend, Susan Collins, then the two of them rowed to the village green. They found James already there with his mum and dad squashed into the dinghy with him. Mrs Hope appeared soon afterwards, ferrying Mrs Ponsonby along.

'This is just fabulous,' boomed Mrs Ponsonby as other villagers began to arrive. 'Well done, Mandy and James. It's just what Welford needed to put us all back into the Christmas spirit.'

Adam Hope appeared from the other direction with Gran and Grandad Hope. They paddled from boat to boat handing out candles which Gran had brought along. 'Just in case any of you had run out by now,' she said cheerfully.

Last to arrive was the punt carrying the choir. 'Seeing as you're going to lead us all in song, you'd better be in the centre of the congregation,' said Andrew Bond, skilfully manoeuvring the narrow punt into the middle of the cluster of boats.

'Goodness me! We even have a full choir,' exclaimed Mrs Ponsonby. 'Now all we need is some music.'

'That's all arranged,' came a voice from a boat alongside the punt.

Mandy turned. 'It's Mrs Davy,' she smiled. 'And she's brought her violin.'

Eileen Davy was a local music teacher. With her were three other musicians, one a guitar player, the other a flautist and the third, Ernie Bell with his accordion.

'Perfect!' Mandy laughed. She looked around her with satisfaction. For the first time in days, the village green was alive with people. 'It looks almost magical,' she told Susan. 'I wish I'd brought a camera.' Mandy realised that Welford would probably never see another picture like it – dozens of little boats floating about the flooded village green in the midst of winter. And in each boat, sparkling candles shimmered in the darkness, making the black water twinkle with bright points of light.

Reverend Hadcroft welcomed everyone to the service. 'In one sense, it's a most unusual way to hold a carol service,' he said. 'But on the other hand, it's really very appropriate. You see, like Mary and Joseph, we're making the best out of a bad situation. They arrived to find the inn full so they had to opt for an alternative. And as we all know, it was a very good one in the end. Likewise, we found ourselves in a tricky situation too, with a flood that looked set to rival Noah's, but thanks to Mandy and James, we have a wonderful solution.'

There were murmurs of agreement all round, then Reverend Hadcroft continued. 'We'll start with *Silent Night*,' he announced.

The musicians played the opening bars then everyone broke into song. One warbling voice soared above the rest. It was Mrs Ponsonby's. And as she sang, she swayed in time to the rhythm. The result was that the boat she was in lurched and rolled, causing Mrs Hope to hold firmly to the sides.

Mandy caught her mother's eye and they exchanged smiles just as the singing came to an end.

'The next carol is *We Three Kings*,' announced the vicar.

The congregation had just started singing when

Mandy noticed something going on at the Fox and Goose. Julian and Sara were standing on the porch, and they seemed to be lighting lots of tiny candles.

'I wonder why they need so many candles?' Susan whispered to Mandy.

'And what's John doing?' Mandy whispered back, noticing him standing a few feet higher in the twilight gloom than Julian and Sara. 'It looks like he's up a ladder.'

'Julian and Sara are passing the candles to him,' Susan pointed out.

'And the candles are in jars with strings tied to them – a bit like lanterns,' Mandy said. She saw John carefully position a jar then bend down to take another candle from Sara. 'It looks like John's hanging them on to something,' she added.

Gradually, as Mandy and Susan watched, the candles that John was placing began to form a triangular outline. Suddenly Mandy realised what was going on. 'They're putting candles on a Christmas tree!' she cried in amazement. Quietly picking up her oars she rowed over for a closer look.

James had seen it too. He paddled over behind

her. 'It must be the original tree that was washed away!' he whispered.

The singers were on the last verse of the carol. Their voices died down in hushed amazement as the tree took shape before them. Only Mrs Ponsonby continued to sing, her loud voice trilling the hymn's closing words.

'So you salvaged the tree after all?' James called out to the Hardys.

'Yes. The water had dropped so much by this afternoon, that it was quite easy in the end,' called John from the top of the ladder. He stretched up to hang the last jar at the top of the tree, then looked down at Mandy and James. 'It's a bit bedraggled, but you can't really notice that in the dark.'

Everyone cheered and clapped.

'Well done, the Hardys,' boomed out Mrs Ponsonby. 'Welford has its Christmas tree once more. Now we can really celebrate!' She turned to the little band and proclaimed, 'Maestros, play on!'

As the music to *Hark the Herald Angels Sing* rang out around the green, Mrs Ponsonby began conducting all the singers with huge sweeping gestures that made her boat rock even more, so that the water slapped against the sides.

'That's what you call rock and roll carols,' whispered Mandy to Susan.

Later, there was another surprise for everyone – a floating picnic which Grandma Hope and her fellow W.I. members had organised. When the singing was nearly over, Gran held up a big wicker basket. 'Mince pies and shortbread for everyone,' she announced. 'But don't all row across at once. The last thing Welford needs now is a tidal wave!'

'And just in case there isn't enough liquid around, there's hot punch in my boat,' added Mrs Ponsonby, taking several big flasks out of a hamper at her feet.

The singers clustered around the two boats, delighted with the refreshments.

'It's very kind of you,' grunted Ernie Bell, after paddling the band across to Gran and Mrs Ponsonby. Then, with unusual gusto, he held up his cup of punch and toasted the congregation. 'Cheers!' he said. 'And Merry Christmas to you all!'

In reply, a rousing cry of: 'Cheers, everyone!' rang out around the village green.

Mandy had just taken a big bite of her mince pie so she simply held up her cup in a silent toast. As she admired the restored Christmas tree again, she glimpsed the flicker of a candle in the window of one of the cottages just beyond the pub. It was Walter's cottage. *Poor Walter*, Mandy thought sadly. *He would have loved this*.

In her mind's eye, she could picture the old man and his cats. She tried not to dwell on the sad scene, but she couldn't push it from her mind. There was such a contrast between the joy all around her and the sorrow that Walter was going through. *At least Mum and Dad are around for Walter*, Mandy comforted herself. *They'll make sure Scraps goes peacefully*.

There was one more surprise for the carollers that night. As everyone began to sing the final carol the clouds drifted apart and a single star appeared – right above the Christmas tree.

'Well! Who would have believed it?' Mandy whispered to Susan. 'There's a star at the top of the Christmas tree after all!'

Back at Animal Ark later that evening, feeling pleasantly full from several mince pies and a glass of hot fruit punch, Mandy went to check on Flicker.

'It's only me,' she said softly, entering the residential unit which was dimly lit with a gas lamp that hung from a hook in one corner. Automatically, Mandy reached for the light switch on the wall next to the door.

'Oops!' she muttered when nothing happened. It was beginning to feel as if the power would never come back on. She unhooked the lantern and swung it towards Flicker's cage.

Flicker's bright green eyes shone out from inside the cardboard box. But this was all that Mandy could see of her. She knelt down in front of the cage and waited silently for a few minutes. Flicker didn't even stir.

'Oh, well,' Mandy sighed, standing up after a while. 'I guess you still want to be left alone. But it's only two days before Christmas. And no one should be miserable on Christmas Day.'

However, as she spoke the words, Mandy knew in her heart that things weren't always perfect – even at Christmas. *Everywhere, there are people who are lonely or hurting at this time*, she told herself as she went out of the unit. *Just like Walter.*

Ten

When the phone rang early the next morning, Mandy knew before she answered it that the caller was Walter Pickard.

'Would you tell your dad that I think the time has come?' he said gruffly. 'I can't let Scraps suffer any more.'

'We'll be there very soon,' Mandy promised him.

She went into the kitchen to tell her mum and dad. Mrs Hope said she'd go round straightaway as Mr Hope was busy catching up with some paperwork. 'It looks like I'll be able to take the Land-rover,' she remarked, looking out at the driveway where patches of tarmac now showed between the puddles.

'I'll go with you,' Mandy offered.

While Mrs Hope fetched her vet's bag, Mandy and her dad dragged the compost-filled sacks away from the garage door. The compost had soaked up a lot of water so the bags were very heavy.

'They did a good job,' said Adam Hope, opening the garage door to find only a very shallow layer of water on the floor.

Mrs Hope came out and put her bag into the Land-rover, then she and Mandy drove off. Even though the water was receding, the village was still pretty empty. Mandy spotted just one person hurrying across the soggy green before her mum turned into the lane to Walter's cottage.

The old man must have been watching for them from his front window because just as they pushed open the gate, he came out of the door. Scraps was lying in his arms.

Mrs Hope took one look at the fragile ginger cat and said quietly, 'You're right, Walter. It's time.'

They went inside where Walter sat down in his

armchair. He cradled Scraps lovingly and whispered huskily, 'You're a champion old lass. We've had some good times, haven't we?' Then, as Mrs Hope prepared the injection that would put Scraps out of her pain, Walter lowered his head. 'Goodbye, Scraps,' he said, kissing the cat's head. 'I'm going to miss you so much.'

Tears welled up in Mandy's eyes and she turned away. Out of the corner of her eye, she saw a black and white blur jumping up next to Walter. It was Tom. He was keeping up his vigil while his old companion drifted peacefully into an eternity of sleep.

'There,' Mandy heard her mum saying softly. 'She's gone now, Walter.'

Mandy turned round again. Walter was staring down at the lifeless little body in his lap. He wiped his eyes with the back of one hand and said gruffly, 'I suppose it was for the best. She couldn't have gone on like that any more.'

Mrs Hope nodded. 'And you were with her right to the end. It's the best we can hope for for our pets – to slip away quietly in their own homes surrounded by those who love them.'

'Aye,' murmured Walter.

'I wish we could explain that to Tom,' Mandy said. 'He's really upset.'

Tom was nudging Scraps's limp, silent form with his nose, as if expecting her to wake up.

Mrs Hope stroked Tom's bony back. 'He'll come to terms with things soon,' she said. 'Then he'll probably start eating normally and put back some of the weight he's lost.'

Mandy and her mum waited for a few minutes, then Mrs Hope offered to take Scraps away to bury her.

'I'll be doing that,' Walter said at once. 'I've got a spot all planned out. I know she'd want to stay in her own garden. But I just want to sit with her for a few more minutes.'

Mrs Hope let her hand rest lightly on Walter's shoulder for a moment before she and Mandy slipped away. As they walked down the path, Mandy glanced back over her shoulder. Tom was sitting in the hall window gazing out forlornly at them.

'Poor Tom,' Mandy whispered, biting her lip to fight back the tears that were still welling up inside her.

'I guess he's terribly confused,' said Mrs Hope.

'Some people say that animals have no sense of mortality. But looking at Tom, I'd say he has.'

They climbed into the Land-rover and Mrs Hope started the engine. She looked across at Mandy. 'Try not to worry too much, love. I'm sure Tom will soon go back to being his normal unfriendly self.'

'I don't know,' Mandy said, shaking her head. 'I've never seen him even slightly upset about anything before. I think he'll take ages to get over Scraps.'

That evening, there was another call from Walter. 'I'm sorry to trouble you so late,' began the old man anxiously when Mandy picked up the phone, 'but it's Tom, you see. He seems so ill. It's not just that he's off his food. He's got no energy in him at all. He's just lying on the floor, staring at the fire.' He paused, then added slowly, 'I think he's going the same way as Scraps.'

Mr Hope came into the hall and Mandy handed him the receiver. He listened to Walter, then said, 'We're on our way.'

Mandy and Mr Hope arrived at Walter's cottage to find Tom looking very frail. 'He's definitely worse than he was this morning,' Mandy said, picking him up. The famously bad-tempered cat didn't even struggle in her arms.

'Let's have a good look at him,' said Mr Hope, opening his bag. 'Put him on the table please, Mandy.'

Tom slumped on to his side when Mandy put him down.

'See what I mean,' said Walter. 'He can hardly hold himself up.'

Mr Hope examined Tom while Walter looked on, his face clouded with worry. At last, Mr Hope took off his stethoscope and turned to Walter. 'He's dehydrated and weak from hunger. But I can assure you it's not because of any disease.'

'It's just because he's pining, is it?' asked Walter.

'That's right,' said Mr Hope. 'I can do something about his physical condition, but to be honest, there's nothing I can do to mend his heart. He'll have to come round in his own time. But for now, we'll take him back to the surgery and keep him on a drip for a day or two.'

Mandy wrapped Tom in a blanket, then she and her dad took him back to Animal Ark.

In the surgery, Mr Hope lit a gas lamp. 'Not the

best light for treating an animal,' he said, putting the lamp on the desk, 'but in the absence of electricity, it'll have to do.' He opened a cupboard and took out a plastic bag filled with an electrolyte solution. 'Let's get some fluid into you, Tom,' he said.

While Mandy held Tom still, Mr Hope inserted a needle into the cat's foreleg. Mandy wrapped some sticking plaster tightly round the leg to prevent Tom pulling the drip out. 'Just shows how weak he is,' she said as they took the docile cat through to the residential unit. 'Normally he'd never co-operate like this.'

They put Tom in a cage next to Flicker.

'Some company for you, Flicker,' Mandy said, peering into her cage.

As before, Flicker just stared out from her box. But as Mandy and Mr Hope were about to leave, the nervous cat crept slowly out and sniffed the air. She caught Tom's scent and froze.

Mandy and Mr Hope waited. Flicker lifted her head and looked around. Silently she padded over to the side of her cage, her body tense and her ears pricked. When she spotted the cat in the next-door cage, her eyes grew wide. Then she suddenly turned tail and scampered back to her safe hiding place in the box.

Mandy shrugged. 'She's a real scaredy-cat, isn't she?' she said to her dad.

'Uh-huh. Not the bravest I've ever known,' agreed Mr Hope. He glanced at Tom. 'In fact, the two of them make a very touching pair, seeing as they're both so unhappy.'

The next day, Mandy decided to check the cats before breakfast, so she dressed quickly and went down to the surgery.

'Now look here, you two,' she said approaching the cages. 'It's Christmas Eve so you'd jolly well better cheer up . . .' She stopped. In front of her was a scene Mandy hadn't expected. Flicker was standing at the side of her cage, her nose pressed against the wire. She swished her tail casually from side to side in a way that made her look almost relaxed, and she was gazing at Tom with obvious interest.

'That's better,' Mandy murmured.

Tom seemed to have turned the corner too. Last night, his eyes were sunken into his head and his neck drooped feebly, but today he was definitely

brighter. From where he lay in the middle of his cage, he returned Flicker's gaze, his eyes wide and clear.

'You look a lot stronger,' Mandy told him. She checked the drip to make sure it was still working properly, then fetched some clean water and fresh food for the two cats.

For the first time since she'd arrived at Animal Ark, Flicker seemed to accept Mandy's presence as she moved around. The little cat sat calmly at the wire, alternately watching Mandy and Tom.

Mandy was tempted to make a fuss of her but decided against it. 'I'll wait for you to come to me,' she said. She put clean litter trays in the two cages then went to the back of the room and watched to see what the cats would do next.

The two continued to gaze at each other for a few minutes. Every now and then, Flicker would walk a few paces back and forth, rubbing herself against the wire. Then she'd stop and stare at Tom again. Once she even miaowed softly and pawed at the wire. Tom, in turn, lifted his head and pricked up his ears.

The longer Mandy watched them, the more her hopes grew. Both cats definitely seemed to have begun to recover. *Now all we need is for you both to start eating,* she thought to herself.

Almost as if she'd read Mandy's mind, Flicker glanced over her shoulder at her food bowl. She yawned and stretched then, with a flick of her tail, padded over to the dish and ate every last scrap of food.

That's brilliant! Mandy told herself happily.

Tom took his turn next. Seeing Flicker enjoying her breakfast must have triggered something in him. As soon as Flicker sat back and started cleaning herself, Tom stretched his scrawny neck towards his dish. Still lying on his side, he took a few mouthfuls of the food. Then he pulled himself upright and slowly ate the rest.

'Good boy,' Mandy breathed.

When he'd emptied the bowl, Tom began licking and nibbling at the sticking plaster on his leg that held the drip in place.

'I wonder if he needs that now?' Mandy asked herself.

She hurried into the kitchen where her mum was opening a heap of post, the first to be delivered in days.

'Tom's eaten a whole dish of food,' Mandy told

Emily. 'So he might not need his drip any more.'

By the time Mandy and her mum returned to the unit, Flicker was pushing against the wire again, prodding it from time to time with her paws as if she was trying to get Tom's attention.

Mrs Hope opened the cage, picked up Tom and examined him. 'He's definitely hydrated again,' she said, gently pinching his skin to show how it sprang back healthily. 'So let's get rid of the drip and trust he'll keep eating now.' She removed the needle and plaster, then put Tom back in the cage.

No longer hampered by the drip, the tom cat moved slowly around his cage, inquisitively sniffing the floor and sides. Flicker watched him intently as he came closer to her. She twitched her tail then dabbed at the wire with one paw.

Tom stopped and waved his tail behind him. Flicker pawed the side of the cage again and miaowed softly before pressing her nose against the wire.

Mandy held her breath. Flicker seemed to be giving out friendly signals. Would Tom respond to her?

Tom sat very still for a few moments then stood up and slowly walked across to Flicker. He reached the wire and the two cats touched noses before sitting down and staring at one another, blinking every now and then.

Mandy was wondering how long they'd keep this up when Flicker suddenly sat up on her hind legs and put both front paws against the wire. In reply, Tom stood up and walked slowly along the side of the cage. When Flicker suddenly flopped down and flipped over on to her back, Mandy was delighted. The cats seemed to be accomplishing for each other what no one else had been able to achieve. 'Flicker's calmed down, and Tom looks like a load's been lifted from him,' she said to her mum. 'Why don't we let them out so they can meet properly?'

'I was just thinking that myself,' smiled Mrs Hope.

Mandy took Tom out and put him down outside Flicker's cage.

'Let's allow Flicker to come out by herself,' Mrs Hope said, opening the door to her cage.

Mandy and her mum took a few steps back then waited. With enormous caution, Flicker ventured out into the open. Tom was still rather weak so he sat down. But he kept his eyes fixed on his new friend. Flicker crept up to him, glancing around timidly. The two cats touched noses again, then Tom rubbed his chin against Flicker's face before licking the top of her head.

Mandy beamed at the pair. 'They're definitely the best medicine for each other,' she said to her mum.

'Walter will be so relieved,' said Emily Hope. 'Let's tell him right away.'

They closed the door behind them and went into the reception area. Mrs Hope dialled Walter's number and told him the good news. 'Why don't you come and visit Tom?' she said. 'I'm sure he'll be thrilled to see you.'

Walter lost no time in coming round to Animal Ark. Mandy had hardly finished eating her breakfast when she saw him sloshing across the soggy lawn in his wellington boots. She hurried out to meet him, then showed him into the residential unit. The two cats were curled up next to each other in Tom's cage.

Walter could hardly believe the change in Tom. 'He's back to his old self,' he declared, smiling.

'Not really,' Mandy said.

Walter's smile disappeared. 'You mean he's still in a bad way?' he frowned.

'Well, he's still quite weak and low in body fat,' put in Mr Hope who'd also come in to see how the cats were doing. 'But what I think Mandy means is that he's a changed character.'

Walter's forehead wrinkled into a deeper frown. 'Changed? How?'

'He just seems so much friendlier,' Mandy said. 'Look how he's allowing Flicker to lie so close to him. It's like he knew she needed a friend.'

'Aye. Just like he needed one too after . . .' He paused then said softly, 'after losing Scraps.' He reached into the cage and smoothed Tom, his big hand also touching Flicker.

The young cat opened her eyes lazily and looked straight into Walter's unfamiliar face. Then she did something that delighted Mandy almost more than anything else so far. She began to purr, a clear sign to Mandy that she was finally coming out of her shell.

At first it was just a faint rumble but as Walter continued to stroke the two cats, the purr grew louder and more intense.

A longing look settled on Walter's face. 'Scraps had a purr just like that,' he said hoarsely.

Walter spent another half an hour with the cats

then gave Tom a final cuddle. The tom cat needed to stay at Animal Ark for another day so that he could completely regain his strength. 'I'll be back for him first thing in the morning,' Walter said in the reception area, adding quickly, 'You don't mind if I disturb you on Christmas Day?'

'Not at all,' said Mrs Hope. 'We wouldn't want you to be without Tom for Christmas.'

'That's kind of you,' said Walter.

Mandy leaned against the window and watched the old man heading back down the driveway. She was really pleased that Tom was going home. 'But what about Flicker?' she murmured to herself. 'Just when she's feeling happy and has found a friend, she's about to lose him.'

Mr Hope overheard her. He came across and put his arm around her shoulders. 'I dare say someone will give her a home eventually,' he said.

'It would be lovely if Walter took her in,' Mandy said quietly.

'Unfortunately, things don't always work out the way we want them to,' said Mr Hope sympathetically. 'Walter won't be ready to take in another cat for quite a while. He needs to get over losing Scraps first.'

'I know,' muttered Mandy, feeling a wave of disappointment for Flicker. 'But perhaps if we persuade him . . .'

'No. This is no time to be pestering Walter,' said Mr Hope firmly.

Christmas morning brought with it a dazzling blue sky and soft, golden sunshine. 'It's just perfect,' Mandy said to her parents over breakfast. 'Except for one thing.'

'What's that?' asked Mrs Hope.

'Flicker and Tom are going to be separated,' Mandy answered glumly.

The moment Mandy dreaded came all too soon. Walter arrived while she was feeding the cats. He waited while Tom ate, then opened the cage. 'Home time, my boy,' he said. 'Missie's going to be glad to have you back. She's been a bit lonely all on her own.'

Mandy caught her mum's eye. Mrs Hope frowned at her and shook her head. But Mandy's main concern was for Flicker. She'd never forgive herself if she didn't at least *try* to keep the two cats together. 'Wouldn't you like to take Flicker home too?' she blurted out to Walter.

'Me?' said Walter, taken aback. 'Oh, I don't think so. It wouldn't be right, replacing Scraps already.'

'You wouldn't be replacing her,' Mandy insisted. 'Nothing can *ever* replace a pet. But you would be helping a cat who really deserves to be happy. And you're the only one she's responded to so far.' Quickly, she outlined what had happened to Flicker.

Walter was surprised to hear all that Flicker had been through. 'You've had a lucky escape, young lady,' he murmured, reaching into the cage and stroking Flicker's head. He fell silent for a minute.

Mandy crossed her fingers, hardly daring to breathe. *Oh, please say you'll have her,* she silently willed him.

'No. It just wouldn't be right,' Walter said finally. 'I can't be forgetting about Scraps so soon.' He stopped stroking Flicker and picked up Tom.

Mandy's heart dropped. 'But you won't ever forget Scraps. And anyway, what about Tom?' she urged.

Walter frowned as he stood up with Tom in his arms. At that point, Mrs Hope stepped in. 'I think Walter's made up his mind, Mandy,' she said. 'And I'm sure Flicker will find a suitable home.'

Mandy turned away, tears stinging her eyes. Flicker was going to be heartbroken. But just as Mandy had given up hope that Christmas would turn out well for Flicker too, Walter cleared his throat. 'I was just thinking . . .' he began, and paused. 'Well, if I know Scraps, she'd want Tom and Flicker to be happy.'

Mandy spun round.

Walter bent down, and reached into the cage again, picking up Flicker. Kindness filled his voice as he spoke. 'Perhaps Flicker should come home with us after all. There's just something about her. Something that makes me think we're meant for her.'

Mandy threw her arms around the old man. 'Thank you!' she cried, hugging both him and the two cats in his arms. She turned and smiled broadly at her parents. 'Now Christmas *will* be perfect,' she said.

Mrs Hope offered to run Walter and the cats home in the Land-rover, but the old man said he'd prefer to walk. 'It's such a lovely day,' he said. 'I could do with a bit of sun on my back. But perhaps Mandy would like to carry one of my cats for me.'

'You bet!' said Mandy.

Soon Mandy and Walter, each with a cat in their arms, set off down the lane. When they came to the Fox and Goose, they saw James and John Hardy in the car park. They were looking up at the fairy lights which had been strung back up along the eaves.

Mandy called out to them. 'Expecting the electricity to come back on soon?' she laughed.

'It has to, eventually,' called back John. 'We thought we'd look on the bright side. That's why James and I put the lights up again.'

James noticed the two cats and came over to Mandy and Walter. 'What's going on?' he asked.

'Flicker's all right now,' Mandy smiled. 'And thanks to Walter and Tom, she's got a new home.'

Mandy could see that James understood at once what had happened. He stroked both cats, then looked at Walter and beamed at him. 'Happy Christmas, Mr Pickard,' he said.

'And Happy Christmas to you,' said Walter.

'May I come and see Flicker settling in to her new home?' James asked the old man.

'Of course,' replied Walter.

The three of them turned into the lane leading

to Walter's cottage. Suddenly they heard a shout from John.

'Hooray!' he cried.

Mandy spun round. The colourful string of fairy lights was glowing brightly all around the eaves of the pub! 'Hooray!' she echoed. 'The lights are on at last.'